JUNE KRAHOLIK

MILTON & HUGO L.L.C.
4407 Park Ave., Suite 5
Union City, NJ 07087, USA

Website: *www. miltonandhugo.com*
Hotline: *1- 888-778-0033*
Email: *info@miltonandhugo.com*

Ordering Information:
Quantity sales. Special discounts are available on quantity purchases by corporations, associations, and others. For details, contact the publisher at the address above.

Library of Congress Control Number: 2024918231
ISBN-13:   979-8-89285-250-0   [Paperback Edition]
                    979-8-89285-249-4   [Hardback Edition]
                    979-8-89285-248-7   [Digital Edition]

Rev. date: 08/02/2024

To those who found their person and to those who still are searching.

CHAPTER 1

Katie looked out from the porch as the waves crashed into the sand, washing up the shore, until they receded back into the sea. She sat drinking her black coffee, before the chaos of the day began. This was her quiet place, the dream she had for so many years. In her fifties, every goal she wanted was accomplished; and for the first time, Katie felt her life had purpose but still felt she was missing something.

As Katie sat in her thoughts, her phone rang.

"Hello."

"So are we getting excited about tomorrow?" said a young female voice.

"Emma, I've already told you. It is just going to be another messed-up situation as always. We are just going for coffee."

"Yeah, okay, Mom, he calls you after eight years, hello."

"Emma, we are friends and have been for almost forty years."

"I got you," Emma said with a smile. "Hey, I got to go, contemporary art calls. I'll call you later."

"Okay, love you, baby girl," said Katie.

"Love you too, Mom," Emma said.

Emma was Katie's daughter. Katie had Emma later in life, so Emma had just graduated high school and was studying fine arts, with hopes of becoming a famous artist one day. Katie had always encouraged Emma to find her purpose and to hold on to everything that meant the most to her. Emma's dad had divorced Katie years earlier, and Katie and Emma stayed connected at the hip until recently when Emma left for college.

Emma's words, "Are you getting excited," rang through Katie's head. Emma knew most of the story, as Katie wanted Emma to have no mystery when she passed. Katie's heart began to beat fast, and she smiled. Her mind began to wander back to the first time she met Aaron. It seemed like a lifetime ago, but it was a permanent imprint in her mind.

Katie was a sophomore in high school. Her parents moved her to South Georgia in middle school. Katie was so mad at her beach life turning into rural Georgia. To top it off, they lived in the woods, no one in sight. To rebel, the first two years in Georgia, Katie got into as much trouble as possible. She got expelled from school, snuck out, drank alcohol, and smoked cigarettes. She ended up grounded more than she wasn't. Katie's parents did let her do one thing—play soccer, which Katie loved; they hoped it would straighten her out.

Her younger brother, Ryan, seemed to fit right in, as if he lived in Georgia for years. He was the good child—the one with the good grades, never got in trouble, and had goody-goody friends. He believed alcohol was bad and cigarettes you shouldn't smoke. When Katie was in her troubled phase, Ryan would not rat her out to her parents but would blackmail Katie into doing what he wanted. Ryan constantly picked at Katie, irritating her until she would either hit him or cry. They were only two years apart, and they were close, but that did not keep him from picking at Katie. He confessed many times he was so glad he was not Katie.

"Katie, a bunch of us are going to hang out this weekend. You coming?" said Andrea.

"No, I'm grounded. My parents aren't going to go for that."

"All right, maybe next time."

"You guys have fun," said Katie.

"You guys? You talk funny," Andrea said as she walked away.

Katie still didn't fit in. She felt like an outcast in the town she was living. Most had accents that she did not understand and would always say, "You aren't from around here, are you?" Katie wasn't popular although she was liked, probably because of all the trouble she had caused for two years. Katie didn't give a damn either way. She was in living hell and couldn't wait to graduate to move back to Florida.

Even though Katie was grounded every day for the last three years, her parents still would allow her to attend school functions. They thought they were safe and away from the kids she once hung out with. Her parents also knew it was a group of kids with adults, a much safer atmosphere.

Katie was actually attending a cookout during the weekend. She didn't tell her friends at school as she thought it was dull, as all of her friends were hanging out without adult supervision. But the cookout gave Katie time away from her house and away from her parents for a few hours. To Katie, it was freedom.

"Katie, are you ready?" her dad called downstairs.

"Yes, I am coming."

Katie had her shoulder-length blonde hair pulled back in a ponytail and was wearing a T-shirt and Umbros, her normal look. It was hot in South Georgia this time of year, and with no ocean breeze, Katie was going to feel comfortable. She barely ever wore makeup, and today was no different. She thought of herself as average, and for being average, she looked about as good as it was going to get in her eyes.

As Katie got in the car with her dad, she placed her seat belt on, and they were off. Katie liked to drive with her dad because he did not freak out as much as her mom did when Katie drove. Katie was excited. Soon she would have her full license, and she could go and come from the house without asking permission. "Lead foot" was one of the many things her dad would call her on several occasions, along with saying "slow down" and "brake, brake, brake." You couldn't tell Katie anything though. She was driving and almost free to drive by herself. As they pulled up to the cookout, excited Katie slammed the vehicle into park before it had rolled to a complete stop. Both Katie and her dad jerked forward. Katie's dad looked at her with fear in his eyes. "What time do I need to pick you up?"

Katie replied, "Five." With that, Katie jumped out and was off to where everyone was standing under a pavilion.

As Katie made it to the pavilion, friends came and greeted her. Katie was liked. She was outgoing and always had a smile on her face, hiding her problems at home underneath her personality. Katie was the girl people came to when they had problems, and she had long ago become "one of the guys" with her guy friends. Katie was just that girl to many, and Katie didn't mind at all.

As Katie was talking, she saw out of the corner of her eye a tall guy with brown hair talking to others. The tall guy looked over at Katie, and Katie quickly turned away when he saw her staring. Katie sat down on a bench and continued to talk as the tall guy came over, sat down, and started talking to others around the table. Katie looked over at the tall guy again out of the corner of her eye and noticed him looking in her direction.

"Katie, do you know Aaron?" one of her friends asked. Katie shook her head, staring over at this "Aaron."

"Katie, Aaron. Aaron, Katie."

They acknowledged each other and continued their conversation with others. As people came and went from the table, Katie and Aaron remained until Aaron finally said, "So you play soccer, Katie?" Katie looked over at him and noticed for the first time his piercing ocean-blue eyes.

Surprised he knew Katie played soccer, she said, "Yes. I've been playing since I was four. Do you play?"

"No, well, I did when I was in England."

"England?" Katie said, surprised on how Aaron ended up in Georgia from England.

Smiling, Aaron said, "My dad is in the military, and he was stationed there."

"Ahh," Katie said, feeling a little embarrassed. She always forgot how a lot of her friends were also implants from all over due to the air force base being in town.

"You want to go for a drive?" asked Aaron, smiling.

"What?" Katie replied, bewildered by the question.

"That's my car. You want to go for a drive?"

Katie looked over to where Aaron was pointing. A blue Mustang was parked in the direction he was pointing.

"Huh, where are we going to go?" Katie asked.

"I don't know. Let's just drive." This was another thing Katie wasn't accustomed to. In Georgia, people just drove around on roads just to drive around on roads. A concept that made no sense to her.

Intrigued, Katie said, "Sure."

With that, the two got up and walked to the blue Mustang. Aaron went to the passenger side and went to open Katie's door.

"I got it," Katie said, reaching for the door.

Aaron, taken aback, smiled and said, "Okay." The two pulled out and drove down the road.

Aaron broke the silence. "You know, Katie, boys do open doors for girls here. Nothing is meant by it. It's just polite. Where did you come from?" Aaron asked Katie.

"I am not used to it, and it is weird. That obvious I'm not from here?" Katie said.

Aaron laughingly said, "You definitely aren't from Georgia."

Katie smiled, looking at his blue eyes again. "I'm from Florida. My parents thought it was a great idea to move to Georgia because my mom had great childhood memories here."

"I take it you did not think this was a great idea."

"Not at all. I miss my friends."

As the two parked on the side of the road, Katie looked at Aaron. He pointed to a large oak tree. Katie looked at Aaron. "You just want to go sit in those people's yard?"

Aaron laughed. "Nobody cares in Georgia. Come on."

Katie got out of the car, looking around as if they were doing something wrong. She headed in the direction of the oak tree Aaron had pointed to. She stopped and waited for Aaron to come around the corner of the car, and once he reached her, Katie realized how much taller Aaron was to her. Katie stood at five feet, while Aaron was way over six feet tall.

"I'm a little taller than you, I think," Aaron said, noticing what Katie was thinking.

"Just a little bit." Katie laughed.

The two settled under the tree and stared at each other. There was something about Aaron Katie was already fond of. He didn't appear to be cocky like the other guys in school, and he had a deep friendly and sweet tone about the way he spoke to her. Although she just met Aaron, he made her feel safe.

Breaking the silence, Katie asked, "What grade are you in?"

"I'm a senior."

"What are you going to do when you get out of school?"

"I'm going into the air force," Aaron said, laughing as Katie should have known. "What are you going to do, Katie?"

"I don't know. Get out of Georgia. I am moving back to Florida."

"To do what?" Aaron asked.

Katie had not thought it through that far; she just knew she wanted out of Georgia. "I really don't know yet. I always wanted to be a veterinarian but just not sure."

"You thought about the military?"

"Yes, but I don't know if I want to move around that much. Plus, I don't like the cold." To that, Aaron laughed, which made Katie smile. She really liked Aaron; she felt comfortable with him for sure.

"So you know you are not staying in Georgia, you are moving back to Florida, but you don't know what you are going to do when you get down there. And you know you don't want to go into the military because you don't like the cold. Anything else?"

Katie started laughing. "No, not at the moment."

With that, the two smiled at each other. Katie and Aaron sat under the oak tree and talked about their lives and dreams. They spoke about their belief in fate and life. They talked so long both were taken aback when they realized it had been a few hours.

Aaron said, "We better get back. I am sure they are wondering where we are."

The two got back into the blue Mustang. This time, Katie allowed Aaron to open the car door for her. When they arrived back, as Katie and Aaron walked up, several of their friends looked at them in disbelief. "Where have you two been?"

Aaron stated, "Talking," to which the friends stated, "Right."

Katie and Aaron sat down at a table and continued to talk. Time stood still between the two. They truly enjoyed talking, and to both of them, nothing else mattered. It was like they had known each other a long time before today. They felt drawn to each other, a bond that both could not understand in that moment.

"Can I take you home?" Aaron asked.

"Sure," Katie said.

As Katie and Aaron got into the vehicle, they looked at each other and smiled. Aaron grabbed Katie's hand, and they headed to Katie's house. Upon arriving, Aaron looked at Katie and smiled. "Would you go out with me next weekend?"

Katie smiled. "Yes, of course." Katie got out and walked toward her house.

Aaron yelled, "See you at school!" Katie waved and kept walking, smiling where Aaron couldn't see. Aaron smiled as Katie walked away and drove off.

As Katie walked into her house, her smile turned to a frown.

"Who was that?" Katie's mom asked.

Katie walked down the hall. "No one. Just a friend."

"I thought your dad was going to pick you up."

"He was, but I got a ride. The cookout was lame."

When Katie got to her room, she closed her door and lay down on her bed. She replayed the conversations she had with Aaron over and over again in her head, trying to remember everything. Every time Katie thought of Aaron's eyes and smile, it brought a smile to her face. *Crap, I really like him.*

Aaron got home, and he went to his room and closed the door. He lay down on his own bed. *This Katie girl*, he thought. When he thought of her, Aaron could only smile. He was crazy about her since Katie had first opened her mouth. He knew he would be leaving after graduation, but they could be friends. She would pass the time until he could leave for the military.

CHAPTER 2

"So how was the cookout?" Dylan asked Katie when he saw her on Monday. Dylan was Katie's first friend since moving, as they both moved to Georgia about the same time. Although they couldn't stand the sight of each other when they first began playing soccer together, they became best friends after they realized they got along pretty well.

Katie smiled. "It was good."

Dylan looked at Katie. "Wait. Did I miss something?"

"No, you didn't. I met this guy."

"You always meet guys. What guy?" Dylan curiously asked.

"Yes, I do, but his name is Aaron."

"Aaron?" Dylan questioned, raising his eyebrow.

"Uggh, yes." Katie began telling the story to Dylan—about meeting Aaron, about leaving with him, and then about him taking her home. She told Dylan about the two doing something on Saturday and about her really liking him.

Dylan listened intently and said, "So you're telling me you left the cookout, went to a location where you guys were by yourself, and you didn't make out with him."

Katie rolled her eyes at Dylan. "No, you idiot. You're such a dude."

Dylan laughed. "Right. We are going to finish this conversation about Mystery Man later." Katie smiled and watched as Dylan walked away.

Katie's thoughts were all about Aaron. She had not talked to him since the cookout and had not seen him at school. Katie wondered if he had lost her number or if he had changed his mind. At lunch during the middle of the week, Katie sat quietly lost in her thoughts. Dylan was talking to all of their friends as he usually did; he was the social butterfly. The whole day she met Aaron had been playing in her mind over and over again. "Katie, right?" Katie looked up to see Dylan and her other friends looking at her.

Katie replied, "I am sorry, what?"

Dylan pulled Katie to the side. "Katie, what is going on with you?"

"Nothing. I'm sorry. I just got a lot on my mind."

"It wouldn't have anything to do with Mystery Guy, would it?" Dylan said, smiling.

Katie replied, "No, I'm good."

Dylan and Katie were talking when Katie caught a glimpse of Aaron. Aaron was talking to a group of older classmates. "That's him," she said to Dylan who looked in the direction Katie was looking.

"That's him?" Dylan said, shocked.

Katie's heart was beating so fast, she could feel it beating, and her breathing began speeding up. As Katie was looking at Aaron, he locked eyes with her. Aaron smiled and started walking toward her. Katie turned to Dylan and said, "Shit," and started walking toward Aaron.

Katie's mind was racing. What would she talk to him about? What would she say? Would they have anything to talk about? All she knew was she better think of something quick because Blue Eyes was walking straight toward her.

When they met, Aaron said, "Hey, you."

Katie replied, "Hey."

"How have you been?"

"Good." Katie knew she needed to think of more than one-word answers fast.

Aaron said, "Did you still want to do something Saturday?"

"Yes, of course, why would you think I didn't?"

"I didn't know if you had a change of heart," Aaron said, pointing in the direction of Dylan who was staring at them.

"Oh no," Katie said. "That is Dylan. He is my best friend. I've known him since I moved here."

"Ah," Aaron said with a grin, waving at Dylan. As the bell rang, Aaron started to walk off. "See you Saturday?"

"Yes. What time, and what are we going to do?"

"I don't know. I will call you, if that is okay?" Aaron replied.

"Okay."

Katie, smiling, walked back over to Dylan. "What?"

"Really, Katie," Dylan replied.

"What?" Katie replied again.

"Did you pick the tallest guy at the school to be crazy about?"

Katie, rolling her eyes, smiling, said, "I'm not crazy about him."

Dylan replied, "Yeah, you are. Never known a guy to make you nervous and speechless. This is going to be fun."

"Shut up, Dylan," Katie said, playfully slapping him.

That night, Katie walked upstairs to talk to her parents. "Mom, Dad, a group of people are going out on Saturday for a few hours. Do you mind if I go?"

Katie's mom immediately replied, "No, we have talked about this—school, soccer, and some school events."

"Mom, this is a school event, and you said you wanted me to hang around new people. These are good kids."

"The answer is no, Katie," her mom replied.

"Mom, come on. I've not got in any trouble, I have good grades, and I play soccer," Katie said.

"We will think about it, but as of now, it is no," replied Katie's mom.

Katie looked at her dad, and he motioned for her to leave the room.

Katie went back to her room upset that she had to figure out how she could meet Aaron on Saturday. She would be in so much trouble if she left with him and they did not know where she was. She did not say she was going with Aaron; she just said a group of friends. She was so angry at her mom. Katie grabbed a book and started reading. It was her escape from the reality of living in Georgia, her family, and dealing with high school. An hour into reading her book, her dad opened her room door. Katie sat up.

"Look, I talked your mom into letting you go," her dad said. "Katie, Jesus Christ, don't get into any trouble. I will never hear the end of it."

"I won't, Dad, I promise," Katie replied.

" I'm trusting you, Katie."

"I know, Dad."

As Katie's dad walked away, Katie thought, *Oh my gosh. This is really going to happen. I am going to get to see Aaron again. This time, only the two of us.* Katie's heart raced thinking of seeing Aaron again, not at school, not with a bunch of people, just the two of them.

As Katie had received the answer she hoped for from her parents, Aaron paced his room. He had Katie's number in one hand and the phone in the other. He couldn't understand why he was so nervous to call Katie. He had just met her, and nothing could happen between the two; he was leaving soon. They were only friends, and it would be dumb of him to be anything more than just friends with Katie. It was just a phone call. His heart began to pound as he dialed the number.

"Katie, an Aaron is on the phone for you!" Katie's mom barked downstairs.

Katie answered the phone. "I got it, Mom." Katie's mom hung up the phone.

"Hello," Katie said.

"Hey, you," Aaron replied.

"Hey, Aaron."

"Tough night?"

"Not really," Katie replied.

"So I was thinking about picking you up at two," Aaron said.

"Okay, that is good. What are we going to do?" Katie asked.

"I don't know. Ride, maybe park somewhere and just talk," Aaron said.

In Katie's head, it sounded questionable; but without any hesitation, she said, "Okay."

The two began to talk, and before they knew it, an hour had passed. They could talk about everything and anything with each other. It was as if they understood each other. Katie and Aaron had never met anyone they felt so close with. Yes, she had boyfriends, but there was something different with Aaron. She didn't understand it; she didn't know Aaron, but on the other hand, she felt she did.

"Katie, it's time to get off the phone," her dad said.

"Yeah, I got to go," Katie said to Aaron.

"Okay. I will see you Saturday?"

"Yep, at two," Katie replied.

"I will see you then," Aaron replied.

"Bye, Aaron."

"Bye, Katie."

The week dragged on for both Katie and Aaron. But finally, Saturday came, and Katie was getting ready. She decided to put her hair down and throw on a little bit of makeup. As she got dressed, she was talking to Dylan on the phone.

"So your mom is letting you go out with Aaron?"

"Well, technically no. She thinks it is going to be a group of people and that it is a school event," Katie replied.

"And he is going to come pick you up, and you guys are going to go drive and just talk?" Dylan replied.

"Yes."

"And, Katie, you think this is a good idea. Why? You don't even know him, Katie," Dylan replied.

"It's going to be fine. He's not like that, Dylan. He is really a good guy."

"Katie, you know I love you, but I am going to tell you this is not a good idea," Dylan replied.

"You are such a goody-goody, Dylan. Live a little," Katie replied, laughing.

Not finding the humor in the situation, Dylan said, "What time is he coming to pick you up?"

"At two."

"Well, call me when you get home so I know not to go looking for you."

"I will. It's going to be fine. Love ya."

"Love ya too," Dylan replied.

Katie looked in the mirror one more time as she thought, *Why am I so nervous?* She didn't care what others, including guys, thought. She was independent and was never going to give up the life that she wanted. Katie didn't know what she wanted to do, but she knew for sure she wanted a career and to be a boss. She knew she did not want to bow down to a guy and live what she called the old-fashioned way. She was not going to have kids and clean the house and wash clothes, and she was damn sure she was not going to have a guy tell her what to do. If she knew all of this, why was she so nervous? Why him?

Katie's little brother was standing at the door when Katie looked over. "Where are you going dressed up?"

"I'm not dressed up."

"Well, you're not as homeless looking as usual."

"Leave me alone, Ryan."

"You're not going to tell your little ole brother where you are going?"

Katie walked to the door and said no before slamming it. Katie could hear Ryan laughing on the other side of the door.

Katie was a tomboy, the girl all the guys would talk to, and they often told her she was "one of the guys." It was her free spirit, her no-nonsense attitude, and her honesty that all the guys liked. It was who she was. Katie was deemed "one of the guys" years ago, and Katie was okay with it. They felt comfortable being disgusting in front of her, and then she would watch the opposite in front of their girlfriends. It was easier when dealing with guys, as Katie was still uncomfortable dating at times. It always felt awkward to her.

Aaron made her feel different though. He made her want to look her best for him. Katie did not understand why Aaron of all people, the guy she just met, could make her want to try for once not to be just "one of the guys." Katie thought to herself, *When he gets to know me, I will be back to one of the guys. That is just how it is.*

Katie's dad appeared at the door. "Katie, Aaron is here."

"Okay, thanks, Dad."

"You look pretty."

"Whatever."

Katie walked to the door. "Bye, Mom. Bye, Dad."

"Be home early," Katie's mom said.

Katie said, "I will," opening the door.

CHAPTER 3

"Hey, Katie," Aaron said as she got in the car.

"Hey, Aaron, what are we going to do?" Katie replied.

"Let's just drive and figure it out."

"Okay," Katie said as they pulled off.

Aaron turned on the radio, and the two listened to the music playing. "Do you like country music?" Aaron asked Katie.

"No, not really. Never heard it until I moved here and lived in this hell." Aaron laughed at Katie's comment.

"Why do you hate it here so much?" Aaron asked.

"I miss my friends."

"Is that the whole story?" Aaron questioned.

Without hesitation, Katie said, "I knew everyone in Florida. I was born there. I had tons of friends. I had a boyfriend in Florida that I had to leave. Here it seems that I don't fit in, that everyone has their own friends that they have had since birth. It seems like the people that get in trouble are the only ones that want to talk to you, or the guys that just want to get in your pants." Katie paused. "No offense."

Aaron smiled. "None taken."

Katie continued, "I feel like there is more to life than high school, more to the world than a group of cliquish friends that want boyfriends and to talk about each other."

"But yet you don't even know what you are going to do when you get out of there," Aaron replied.

"No, not yet, but I know I am getting out of here." Katie got quiet. Why had she just told Aaron everything she had held in since she moved? She had only spoken to Dylan previously about her hate for Georgia. But yet here she was sitting next to Aaron, a country boy in Georgia whom she had just met.

Aaron finally broke the silence. "Well, Katie, since you are getting out of here as soon as you can, why don't you try and make the best of it while you are here?"

Katie looked over at Aaron and said, "Okay."

Aaron looked at Katie and smiled. "By the way, I'm not trying to get in your pants, just for the record." Katie began to laugh.

Katie and Aaron drove around listening to music, asking all of the basic questions about siblings, favorite colors, places they had been and people they had dated. Up and down dirt roads they drove before Aaron pulled over to a secluded spot in the middle of the woods. *Oh shit*, Katie thought. *Here we go. This is about to be bad, oh my gosh.* Katie and Aaron turned toward each other.

Aaron, feeling Katie's emotion, took her hand. "We are just talking." Katie smiled with Aaron's words, and for some reason, it calmed her, and she trusted his words.

As the two spoke, Aaron watched as Katie spoke with passion. He saw her light up talking about the life she had before Georgia and the things she had done. All Aaron could do was stare and watch Katie. Katie nervously would look at Aaron, and when she made eye contact with him, seeing him look at her would make her look away. As if there was something forbidden in the way he was looking at her. Katie continued to talk nervously as Aaron just watched.

"Why aren't you saying anything?" Katie finally asked.

"I'm just looking at you and listening," Aaron said as he ran his fingers through her hair. Katie stared back at Aaron; and in her head, she thought, *Kiss me, Aaron.* As if Aaron heard her, he leaned toward Katie, placing his forehead on Katie's forehead; and the two both closed their eyes. Aaron, still running his fingers through Katie's hair, slid his hand on the side of her face as he gently kissed Katie's lips. Katie slid her hands to Aaron's shirt, grabbing on to it tightly as they kissed. Katie's and Aaron's hearts raced as they kissed, only stopping to look at each other and smile. Awkward silence followed before Aaron kissed her lips one more time and then pulled away.

Aaron broke the silence. "Well."

All Katie could say was "Yep." That kiss was everything to Katie. An emotional surge that she had never felt before. She was lightheaded, and she did not know if it was from the kiss or the fact she was breathing so hard.

Aaron was the first to talk again. "So tell me what's up with your mom and you."

"That is a long story," Katie replied to Aaron.

"Well, I have time."

With that, Katie slid across the truck seat, laying her head in Aaron's lap as she began to tell Aaron. Aaron started running his fingers through Katie's hair. "My mom is my mom. She thinks I'm going to turn out in trouble or in jail. My sister is in prison." She waited for Aaron to get awkward after what she had just said.

Aaron replied, "For what?"

Katie began telling Aaron the story of what happened with her sister and the unfolding of the hurricane that was the turning point of moving to Georgia. Aaron listened intently and continued to run his fingers through Katie's hair. He was starstruck by Katie, listening to everything Katie had already been through in the short time that she was alive.

Katie told Aaron about all of the troubles she got into when they first moved to Georgia. "When my sister went to prison, I didn't know that people actually went to prison. I mean, I knew they did, but I thought it was really evil people that went, and she wasn't evil. Like she made a bad decision, but she was a good person." Katie went on to describe the emotional roller coaster she experienced, turning away from the only people who were willing to accept her, the bad kids, to change for the better. The bad kids who, once they saw it on the news, kept talking to her and didn't shy away from her. Katie explained to Aaron the persona she had put in place to protect herself from those who did not know about it and those who were only trying to be her friend because of the wrong reasons.

"It was as if all of the people that were 'good' expected me to end up in the same place." Katie told Aaron that she guarded herself from everyone and did not let anyone in, protecting herself from those who one day would react negatively toward her. "It's like I have all these expectations of the daughter I should be too. My mom is always so mean with what she says to me. She doesn't do it to my little brother, but it is like I am the target. I've changed. The whole situation made me realize I did not want to end up like that. I want to be different." Katie paused. "Do you think we are destine to end up like our family, to make the same mistakes?"

Aaron said, "Katie, I think we all make our own decisions. I would like to believe we won't end up as some of our family members. I think that life is what we make of it, and what we choose sometimes is wrong and other times is right. Life is about choices. But to answer your question, no, I don't think you're going to end up like your sister. I sure hope not anyway."

With that, Katie smiled. "Do you believe in love, Aaron?"

The question took Aaron by surprise. "Huh, yes, I guess. What about you?"

"I believe that there is one person for everyone. That once you meet them, you know and that the two are perfect together. Like they were meant to be together, that they were put here for each other."

"Ah, you are a dreamer, Katie. I don't think love is that simple."

"So you don't believe in love?"

Aaron stated, "Yeah, I believe in love, but I don't think it is as simple as you make it out to be."

Changing the subject, Katie said, "You know, you have beautiful eyes."

Aaron laughed. "Oh really."

Katie smiled. "Yes, blue eyes." They both stared at each other, Katie still laying her head in his lap and Aaron running his fingers through her hair.

"So tell me something about you," Katie said.

"Something about me?" Aaron questioned.

"Yes, something that a lot of people don't know," Katie replied.

Aaron, without hesitation, told Katie that he lived with his mom, sister, and brother. He told her about the divorce between his parents and how his dad moved away. Aaron felt as if he had to take care of his mom, brother, and sister. Aaron felt that the military was his way to see the world. Given that his grandfather and father were both in the military, it was inevitable that he was going in the military as well, which he did not mind at all.

Aaron and Katie continued to talk as it began to get dark outside. Both took turns telling each other pieces of their life, pieces they shared with no one else, each trusting their worst and best of times were safe with the other.

"We better go, Katie," Aaron said finally. "You can't be late."

Katie, rolling her eyes, lifted her head from Aaron's lap. She looked at Aaron and kissed his lips one more time. "Okay," she said, pulling away.

Aaron put his fingers through Katie's hair one last time.

Katie took her hand and started to trace Aaron's face with her fingers.

"What are you doing?" Aaron asked while closing his eyes.

"I want to remember every inch of your face," Katie said, smiling.

"Really."

"Yes, really." Katie pulled away and sat back in the seat laughing.

"Are you finished?" Aaron asked, amused.

"Yep, I'm good now."

Aaron smiled, looking at Katie; Katie intrigued him. She was different from so many other girls he had met. As they pulled up to Katie's house, Aaron and Katie turned and looked at each other.

"I had fun tonight," Katie said.

"Fun driving dirt roads and parking?"

Katie smiled. "Yes, and being with you."

Aaron smiled and leaned toward Katie, kissing her lips one last time. "Good night, Katie," he stated.

"Good night, Aaron."

Katie walked inside, wiping every bit of smile off her face.

"How was tonight?" her dad asked.

"It was good," said Katie.

"What did you guys do?"

"Nothing much, just talked really," Katie said, shrugging her shoulders. "It was good."

"Well, that's good."

Katie went to her room and closed her door. She went over her conversation with Aaron, wanting to remember every detail. Of course, in doing so, she remembered the kiss—the kiss that made her lightheaded. She felt like she had known Aaron forever and that there was something different about him. She felt so close to him, like she could trust him, and she felt so safe. Katie just knew there was something special that they shared together. Did she really know him though? How could she like someone so much already?

"Is Aaron you boyfriend?" Katie heard her little brother tease.

"Leave me alone."

"Did you kiss him?"

"Leave me alone, Ryan."

"Do you tell him you love him?"

Katie had enough; she got up from her bed and closed the door, leaving Ryan to laugh hysterically at the irritation he caused Katie. Love, no, she couldn't love him; but she knew she really liked him. It was like no amount of time was long enough with him.

———————————

When Aaron entered his house, it was empty. He walked to his room and closed the door, smiling to himself. What was going on with him? He would be leaving soon, and he knew he would have to leave Katie behind. He knew that Katie would have to finish high school, and it would be impossible to get her to move anywhere but back to Florida. With all of his plans looming, he did not care. All Aaron knew was Katie was special, not like the other girls, and he wanted to spend every minute he could with her until he left.

CHAPTER 4

Katie picked up the phone and dialed Dylan as she said she would.

"So did you sleep with him?" Dylan asked.

"Jesus Christ, Dylan, no," Katie replied, irritated at the question.

"So you went driving with a senior, parked for hours in an area, where no one could see the two of you, and you didn't screw him?"

"No, Dylan, it's not like that," Katie replied.

"What the hell did you guys do the whole time then?"

"We just talked about everything."

"Just talked?" Dylan questioned.

"Yes."

"And next you're going to tell me you didn't kiss him."

"No, we did kiss."

"How was that?"

"Why are you wanting to know all of this? It was awesome." Katie's face lit up thinking of the kiss she and Aaron had shared.

"Awesome?" Dylan questioned.

"Yes. Goodbye, Dylan."

"You going to leave me hanging?" Dylan said.

Katie hung up the phone.

It was different between Aaron and her. Dylan was right about that. They just enjoyed each other's company and being with each other. *Did you sleep with him?* rang through Katie's head. That was the furthest from her mind and she felt Aaron's mind too. It was more about being next to each other than sexual. Katie didn't know why; they were teenagers, but it was just different—the only words Katie could use to describe it.

Katie's parents could see a change within Katie the next few weeks. They had lightened up on Katie and allowed her to see Aaron. Their once-happy child had found her happiness again. Her happiness lay within Aaron, and they knew Katie would be crushed once Aaron left. Katie's parents liked Aaron; he was a "good kid," as they called him. Watching them together, whether Katie and Aaron knew it or not, her parents knew they were in love.

"George, this is not going to work," Katie's mom said one night.

"He is going to be gone soon, Sharon. Let them have fun while he is here."

"And we will have to pick up the pieces when he is gone."

"We are not going to be able to keep them apart, Sharon. Look at them."

Katie and Aaron were sitting on a swing on the front porch, rocking back and forth, just talking. Katie had her head in Aaron's lap, Aaron was running his fingers through Katie's hair. Both were smiling and laughing.

"I just don't want to see her get hurt."

"I don't either, but it's going to happen. We will be here when it does. Katie hasn't been this happy in a long time. Let her be happy while she can, Sharon. You don't know, it may work out in the end."

Katie's mom snapped, "It won't. They are too young."

With that, Katie's dad said no more. Katie's mom was always negative about boyfriends and girlfriends the kids had while in school. When

George tried to ask questions on why, it always ended in a heated discussion with Sharon. George knew the subject was off-limits.

"What do you think is going to happen to us in the future?" Katie asked Aaron as they swung on the porch.

"I don't know. I don't like to think about it. I'm here now."

"I just keep thinking about it, wondering what is going to happen to us with you gone to boot camp and being stationed somewhere else," Katie said with a break in her voice.

"I'm going to call you every chance I get, and I will be home as much as possible. Plus, maybe I can talk your mom into letting you come stay with me for a weekend."

"Yeah, my mom doesn't like you that much," Katie said, laughing.

"Katie, let's just not think about it and be together as much as possible. I really don't want to think about it right now, to tell you the truth."

Katie saw out of the corner of her eye her little brother. "Awww, aren't you two so cute."

Katie, feeling the anger, stated, "Go away." Aaron began to laugh at Katie and her little brother arguing. As her little brother began making kiss noises, Katie sat up. When she did, her little brother ran inside.

She laid her head back in Aaron's lap, and the two continued to talk on the swing.

As Aaron looked at Katie, he was trying to keep it together; but inside, he was torn. He knew the time was coming to leave Katie for his adult life. Aaron knew he would also be crushed when he left. He only downplayed the situation because he wanted to be strong for Katie. He would be just as heartbroken as she.

Weeks went by in the blink of an eye. Before the two knew it, it was graduation and the night of Aaron's graduation party. Katie was in her room getting ready. She knew the days were getting closer, but the fact that tonight was the last night she would see Aaron started to weigh heavy on her mind. The year was like a fairy tale. Katie had found her person, and she knew it. Her heart was already breaking, and there was nothing she could do about it.

Katie stood and looked at herself in the mirror. This past year had changed her; Aaron had changed her. She had traded her T-shirt and Umbros for a pair of jean shorts and a feminine blouse. Her hair was down, and she had makeup on. She didn't see the tomboy in the mirror that was once there. Instead, she saw a woman who loved a man more than anything. Aaron was her other half; he was her soulmate.

The whole year was filled with so many memories for Katie—all of the drives, the dances, and the times they spent together, just the two of them. It was always the two of them, and neither wanted it any other way. They were connected and trusted each other. They knew the other was their safe haven from the world. They knew it, but everyone else said they were too young to know if what they had was special.

As the phone rang, Katie picked it up. "Hello."

"So are you going to sleep with him tonight?" It was Dylan. It had become his best dig at Katie. He thought the whole situation strange as much as the two cared for each other. He did not understand as teenagers how just spending time together meant more than sex.

"You really annoy me, you know that?"

Dylan laughingly said, "I am joking. I just wanted to let you know I am here if you need me." Katie had already cried to Dylan about Aaron leaving. Dylan knew Katie was devastated, and he knew this would be the last time she would see Aaron.

Being strong and acting as if it didn't bother her, she said, "Thanks, Dylan, we really don't want to think about it. We just want to have a good time and be ourselves with each other tonight. Tomorrow is another day."

"I know, Katie. Just know I am always here," Dylan stated.

"Thanks, Dylan." Katie hung up the phone. She stared in the mirror for a long time. Tonight was the last night she would see Aaron. They decided it would be too hard for both of them to see him off. They decided together that he would go with his family, without Katie. Katie's eyes filled with tears. She took a deep breath and choked back the tears when she heard her mom yelling downstairs, "Katie, Aaron is here!"

As Katie walked toward the door, her little brother popped his head out of his room. He looked at Katie. "You are dressed like a girl."

"No shit, I am a girl."

Her little brother started making kiss sounds as she walked upstairs. Katie shot him a bird and kept walking.

Katie got in Aaron's car and shut the door. She had since choked back the tears, but Aaron could feel it. He could see it in her eyes. Aaron looked at Katie and felt her pain; his eyes began to water. "Katie, we can't do this."

"I know," Katie replied.

"Let's just not think about it, okay?"

"Okay."

Aaron leaned over and kissed Katie, placing his forehead against hers. "I love you."

"I love you, Aaron."

At the graduation party, everyone was celebrating; everyone was so excited for Aaron. They were excited about the future he would have and being able to travel the world while he was young. There was drinking, there was food, and there was a bonfire. Everyone was excited for Aaron. They both smiled and laughed about past times and even the future and the excitement that awaited them, but it was with a heavy heart. After people had left and only a few family members remained, Aaron sat down by the bonfire, and Katie sat in the chair beside him. Both were silent looking at the fire.

Aaron looked over at Katie. "Come here." Katie got up and walked to Aaron, curling up in his lap and putting her head on Aaron's chest. He wrapped his arms around Katie, and they both sat in silence watching the fire in front of them. They wanted to soak in the last few hours before Katie had to leave.

"Ask your mom if you can stay with me tonight."

Katie looked at Aaron. "She really doesn't like you that much."

Aaron started grinning. "It doesn't hurt to ask."

Katie dialed her number. "Mom, it's pretty late. Do you mind if I stay over here tonight with Aaron? His family is here, and I don't want to come home yet." Katie mouthed "oh my god" to Aaron. Aaron just smiled. "Okay, Mom, love you too. Bye."

Aaron looked at Katie, waiting for an answer. Katie looked up after hanging up the phone.

"She said yes. What the hell."

Aaron said, "I told you she liked me."

Katie smiled. "She doesn't like you that much."

"Let's lie on the floor." Katie looked at Aaron in surprise. "Just to talk."

Aaron grabbed pillows and a blanket, and the two lay down on the floor together. Katie laid on Aaron's chest with one leg resting on his body. Aaron began to caress Katie's back. Both were silent for a while.

"When are they taking you to the airport?"

"We are going to leave tomorrow, so we don't have to get up so early. I fly out of Jacksonville at 5:00 AM," Aaron said. "What are you going to do tomorrow?"

Katie's voice broke. "I don't know. I'm really going to miss you, Aaron. I don't want to be here without you."

Aaron closed his eyes, fighting back tears seeing Katie get upset. "It's only a little while, Katie. I am going to call you when I can, and once I get out of boot camp, I can come home on leave and see you. We will keep doing that until you graduate, and then you can come stay with me, wherever I am stationed at. We are going to be okay, Katie."

"But what if it's not? What if you get up there and you have another life and you find someone else?" Katie's eyes began to tear up.

Aaron pulled back from Katie so he could look her in the eyes. "Katie, there will never be anyone like you. No one could take your place." Aaron kissed Katie's lips and pulled away to hold on to her.

The two were quiet for a few moments, and Katie broke the silence. "Hey, have I ever told you I loved you?"

Aaron smiled as this was one of the things they would joke about. "Yes. Have I ever told you I loved you?"

Katie replied, "Yes."

Aaron and Katie closed their eyes, taking in the moment, and the two fell asleep locked in each other's arms.

When Katie woke up, Aaron was still holding on to Katie in the same position they fell asleep in. When Katie moved, it woke Aaron up. "Good morning, Katie."

"Good morning."

"I could get used to that," Aaron said.

"Well, buddy, you are leaving today. So if you want to do that again, just don't go," Katie joked with Aaron.

Aaron grabbed Katie and kissed her. "You need to go home, don't you?"

Katie looked at Aaron. "Yes, we are lucky I got to stay."

"I told you your mom liked me."

"She doesn't like you that much, Aaron. But for some reason, she trusts you."

"I am a good guy," Aaron said, looking at Katie. Katie just rolled her eyes.

Both got up off the ground, picked up the pillows, and folded the blanket. They were trying to waste time just to spend those few moments they had left together.

The ride to Katie's house was quiet. Hand in hand, Aaron watched the road as Katie looked out the window. When Aaron pulled up in Katie's driveway, he placed the vehicle in park and looked at Katie. As Katie looked at her house, tears started to form in her eyes. She turned to Aaron who was looking at her.

"Katie, we said we weren't going to do this." Katie could not contain the tears anymore. She threw her arms around Aaron's neck and cried.

Aaron's voice cracked. "Katie, it's going to be okay." Aaron was trying to console Katie. "We are going to be fine. We always got each other, okay?" Aaron wiped Katie's tears before pulling her hair away from her face. He cupped her cheek in his hand. "I love you, Katie. Nothing is ever going to change that."

Katie gave Aaron a half smile. "I love you too, Aaron."

"You got to stop this, Katie," Aaron said.

Katie took a deep breath and said, "I know. I'm kinda gonna miss you though."

Aaron kissed Katie's forehead for the final time. "Me too."

Katie took in Aaron's blue eyes for the last time she knew for a while. "I'll talk to you later."

"Yeah, of course," Aaron said with a smile.

Katie got out of Aaron's car and watched as he pulled away. Waving to Aaron. Katie began crying again and walked inside, never looking up from the ground. Katie's mom was standing in the kitchen when Katie walked in. She could see how upset Katie was, and she could feel her heartbreak.

Katie's mom's eyes began to well up with tears. "Do you want to talk about it?"

Katie walked down the hall. "No."

Katie's mom watched her walk down the hall until she had entered her room and shut the door. Katie's mom sat down in a chair and began to weep for Katie.

Katie's dad, not knowing the turn of events, walked into the room. "Is Katie home?"

When he saw his wife's face, he stopped. "Sharon, what's wrong?"

Katie's mom, crying, mustered out, "George, our baby's heart is broken."

George hugged Sharon with tears in his eyes and began to rub Sharon's back, comforting her. "It's going to be alright," he said.

"But is it, George?"

"We will figure it out."

Katie made it to her room and lay down on her bed. She put her hands over her eyes and began to cry uncontrollably. Her little brother walked into her room and sat at the side of her bed. "Katie, are you okay?"

Katie replied, "No." Her little brother said nothing else but sat at the edge of Katie's bed so she didn't have to be alone.

———————————————

As Aaron got home, it hit him all at once. He looked around his room. It would be the last night he would be there. He would be leaving everything that he knew to follow his dreams and in his grandfather's and dad's footsteps. This is what he always wanted going through school. He knew this was what his life was meant to be, to serve his country. He always wanted to be a soldier, but at a time when he felt his life was beginning, his heart was heavy. He didn't want to leave Katie behind. If only she could go with him, things would be exactly the way they should be. Aaron laid back on his bed. He began to reminisce on all the memories he had with Katie. Aaron put his hands over his eyes to stop himself from tearing up, but it didn't help. He was heartbroken.

CHAPTER 5

That summer, Katie would spend her day working, and her night would be spent thinking of Aaron. She heard from Aaron a few times but not enough. She was trying to get used to the new normal, but being so young, it was hard. Katie kept pushing though, knowing Aaron would come home soon.

If Katie wasn't working, she was playing travel soccer, at practice or games. It kept her mind off things, and it gave her time to talk to Dylan.

"Katie, you really need to get out more. All you are doing is working. Why don't you come out with us tomorrow? The summer is ending soon. Let's have fun."

"No, I'm good, Dylan," Katie said with a half smile. "I want to be home in case Aaron calls. You know that."

"Katie, you can't stay inside waiting for a phone call that may or may not come," Dylan replied.

"I know, Dylan. I'm just not ready."

With that, Katie left Dylan where he was standing and walked away. Dylan missed Katie; she was his best friend. She was not herself since Aaron had left, and Dylan knew there was nothing he could do for her. His heart broke for Katie, and he just wanted his friend back.

Aaron had changed Katie in many ways, and Dylan knew it. Aaron had opened Katie's heart and mind to the world. He gave her hope for the future, and he loved her for who she was. Aaron had made Katie feel beautiful, and Katie had grown so confident—something Dylan knew Katie struggled with before Aaron. He watched as Katie transformed from the tomboy he once knew into a confident woman. Now, his friend's happiness lay in phone calls.

"Hey, you."

"Hey, Aaron, what are you doing?"

"Well, we have a few minutes, so I decided to call you," Aaron said.

"I miss you, Aaron."

"I miss you too, Katie."

"How is boot camp," she asked Aaron.

"It's alright. I am ready to have this behind me."

"I bet. Do you know where they are going to station you yet?"

Aaron had dreaded that question and was holding off on telling Katie. "Yeah, I am going to be in North Dakota."

"North Dakota?" Katie said in shock.

"Yeah, that is going to be my first station. But after my tech school and boot camp, I will get to come home for a few days before going to North Dakota." Aaron was trying to make the bomb he had just dropped on Katie better.

"Yeah, that's good," Katie replied, trying to take in the news she had just heard.

The two talked a few more minutes before Katie heard yelling in the background.

"What is that?" Katie asked.

"I got to go, Katie. I love you."

"I love you too, Aaron."

Katie heard the phone click, and Aaron was gone. She sat on her bed thinking about what Aaron had just told her. North Dakota, really? She had dreams of Aaron being stationed a few hours away and him coming and surprising her on the weekends. Or she could jump in the car and spend a week or weekend together. North Dakota, Katie didn't know how far away it actually was, but it was far, and it was cold there.

Why did it seem like no matter what, everything kept pulling them farther away? Like no matter what they did, how hard they tried, they never could make it work. Now they would never see each other. How were they going to make it work if they could never see each other? *Life just isn't fair*, Katie thought. *It isn't meant to be like this.* She wanted to dream of a happy ending but did not know how to get over all the obstacles in their way. Katie picked up the picture that she and Aaron had taken together. "Come back to me," Katie whispered. "I'm here waiting for you."

———— •— —• ————

"North Dakota, what the hell!" Dylan said in shock.

"Yeah, it sucks."

"What are you going to do?" Dylan questioned, knowing Katie did not like the cold.

"There isn't anything I can do right now. I guess we are going to keep going the way we are until we can see each other. There isn't much I can do until after graduation anyway. Hopefully after graduation, maybe he will be stationed somewhere else."

"Yeah," Dylan said, not convinced that Aaron and Katie were going to make it. He knew they loved each other, even at their age, but he did not see Aaron waiting on Katie for two more years. Aaron was an adult now, doing adult things, going out with the guys, Dylan was sure. If only Dylan could get Katie to leave the house and just live a little. As many times as Dylan tried, Katie always refused to go, hoping that she would hear from Aaron.

As luck would have it, a few weeks later, the phone rang. "Hello," Katie said.

"Katie, guess what? I graduated!" Aaron excitedly said on the other end.

"That's great, Aaron. Congratulations, I am so proud of you."

"Some of us are going to go out and celebrate. I just wanted to call you really quick."

"That will be great. Who all is going out?" Katie said curiously.

"Just some people I met. I will call you later?"

"Okay, I will talk to you then."

Aaron could hear the emotion in Katie's voice, "Hey . . . Katie, I love you."

"I love you too," Katie replied.

"You are in my heart. Things are going to be okay," Aaron replied with complete honesty.

"I know."

"Bye, Katie."

"Bye, Aaron."

Katie knew she could not worry about Aaron. She knew he needed to experience and live life. Aaron had entered a new exciting time in his life. He was an adult, and it was freedom that he never had before. Aaron was living on his own, in another place, doing what he dreamed of, and making money. She had faith most days that their love would always keep them together. Katie did not know how, but she just felt it deep inside her.

Katie spent the rest of the summer working and talking to Aaron as much as possible. She was dreading going back to school without Aaron being there. She had two more years, and then she could be with Aaron. When school started again, Katie's worst fears became a reality. Everywhere she looked, it reminded her of Aaron. Every crevice in the school had a memory to remind her of him. Soon would come the dances and the cookouts. Katie would be alone, holding on to hope of one day.

This year was made even worse by Dylan's parents moving to another town. It meant Dylan changed schools, and Katie could not lean on him as she had since Aaron was gone. The two were reduced to phone calls and meetups on the weekend, but since Dylan had a girlfriend now, it was almost impossible to have the time with him Katie once had. She still had other friends, but she kept her distance from them. They did not understand, and she did not want to explain the complicated relationship that she was in.

Katie continued to follow her routine. She would get up every day, go to school, go to work, and come home to wait for Aaron's phone call. Katie's parents urged her to go out on the weekends and do things, but Katie never would. She sat and waited for Aaron to call; and if Aaron did not call, Katie would bury herself in a book, dreaming of a better ending than what she was living at the moment with Aaron.

"Katie, Aaron is gone," her mom snapped. "You need to move on and live your life. I'm tired of you moping around here when you can be out doing things with your friends."

Katie thought, *How things have changed. Before, I could not do anything and was grounded. Now she is wanting me to get out of the house with friends. Not even with adults. You would think she would be happy she didn't have to worry about me. But no, I got this wrong too.*

"Mom, I am not moping around. I'm just waiting for Aaron to call. I'm fine."

"You actually think he is waiting for you. He is out doing things with his friends, Katie."

Aggravated Katie said, "He is waiting for me."

"I hope you are not that naive, Katie. Give me a break."

Katie walked off. She could not handle her mom at that moment. She went downstairs and closed her door. Why did no one understand what she and Aaron had? Why was everyone wanting her to move on? What they had was different; it was going to last. Aaron would not do that to her; he loved her.

The phone rang, and Katie picked it up.

"Hey, you," the voice on the other end said.

Katie immediately relaxed. "Hey, Aaron, I've been thinking about you."

Aaron could feel the tension in Katie's voice. "Oh really. What's wrong?"

"Nothing is wrong. Just missing you." Katie did not want to discuss it. Aaron was the most important thing at the moment.

Aaron laughed, but it was short-lived. "Katie, I got to tell you something."

Katie's heart began beating fast. She thought to herself, *Oh my gosh, he found someone else. He is leaving me. This isn't happening. This is a dream.* "What is it, Aaron?"

"Okay, wow, this is so hard to tell you." Aaron paused.

Katie's mind raced. Here it was; he had found someone else and was breaking up with her.

"Are you dating someone else?"

"What? No. Damn, this is hard."

"Oh my god, Aaron, just tell me." Katie was anticipating the worst.

"Katie, I'm getting deployed."

"What does that mean, Aaron? Like for a couple of weeks or something?" Katie questioned.

"No, Katie. I am being sent overseas. I don't know for how long right now, but it will be six months to a year."

"Will we be able to talk? Will you be able to come home on leave at all?"

"I don't know yet, Katie, but we will be able to write letters."

"Letters, like send-letters-to-an-address letters?"

"Yeah."

Katie took a deep breath. It was better than Aaron breaking up with her but another push from the universe. "Well, I will write you every day you are gone," Katie finally said.

Aaron laughed; Katie had taken it better than he expected. "A letter every day, huh?"

"Yep, every day, and I will wait by the phone."

"Katie, it will be in the middle of the night that I will be calling you because of the time change."

Katie laughed. "I will wake up every time you call."

"Oh really, you think?" Aaron joked, knowing Katie was a deep sleeper.

Katie laughed. "I will sleep with the phone right next to my pillow."

Both became silent, not knowing what else to say.

Aaron finally spoke. "Have I ever told you I love you?"

Katie smiled. "Yes, have I ever told I love you?"

Aaron said, "Yeah, you have."

"When do you leave?" Katie asked.

"I don't know exactly yet, but maybe around three weeks."

"I am really going to write you every day while you are gone."

Aaron laughed. "We will see about that."

Katie and Aaron continued to talk about everything but Aaron's upcoming deployment. Aaron told Katie about his job and the friends he had made. He told Katie about how cold it was there and how much Katie would have to snuggle with him to stay warm. Katie agreed that would be the perfect way to stay warm with Aaron. She longed to sleep next to Aaron again. To have him kiss her forehead and run his fingers through her hair. She missed looking into his blue eyes that she had fallen in love with.

"I miss you, Katie," Aaron whispered.

"I miss you, Aaron."

Katie had no idea how much Aaron missed her. He thought about her constantly throughout the day. He daydreamed about the life that one day he hoped to give Katie. He just needed Katie to hold on for a little longer. Aaron did not want to tell Katie to wait for him. He always felt that it was his choice to leave, and he wanted Katie to be happy no matter what her choice was. The truth was, Aaron could not see life without Katie in it.

"So he's being deployed," Dylan said.

"Yes."

"Like another country deployed?" Dylan questioned.

"Yes."

Dylan began to laugh. "Man, Katie, he went to North Dakota, and that wasn't far enough away from you. Now he is switching countries."

Katie smiled at Dylan's jab. "Shut up."

"How does that work? Do you get to talk to him?" Dylan asked.

"He will be able to call some but mostly letters."

"Like written mailed letters? Like take-weeks-to-get-here letters?"

"Yes."

"Wow."

"Yeah, that was what I was thinking, but there is nothing I can do."

"Are you sure you still want to do this, Katie? I mean, this is pretty crazy, you know?"

"I love him, Dylan."

"I know, but do you think that maybe when you get out of school, things would be easier?"

Katie cut Dylan off. "No, I want Aaron and only Aaron."

"Okay, we got to make it through out of the country now."

Katie sighed. "Yeah."

"Well, at least when he does get back to North Dakota, it will seem closer."

Katie laughed. "You are such an ass."

Dylan smiled. "I know."

Aaron left three weeks later, but he couldn't tell Katie to which country he was headed to. She only had a generic address to send letters to. Once the letters got to the generic address, they would be separated and sent to where Aaron was. Katie promised Aaron a letter a day, each day that he was gone. She was going to keep her promise.

CHAPTER 6

Aaron,
Hey, you, I miss you already. Today was
a bore at school. My mom is still my
mom wanting me to be someone I am
not. I just don't get it. I got another cat;
I named her Cali. She is so cute. I can't
wait for you to see her. You will love her.
Soccer is starting soon. I can't wait but
am not looking forward to conditioning.
I am doing good in school, just ready to
get out.
Did I ever tell you I love you?
I better go. I have to do my homework. I
will write tomorrow.

Love Always,
Katie

Aaron,
How are you doing? I haven't heard from
you, and I am wondering what you are

up to. I miss you, and I'm ready for you to come home. Well yes, home, but at least to the United States. I wish I could hug you and kiss you. I wish I could look into those eyes of yours forever. Do you miss me, 'cause I miss you. When are you coming home? I hope soon.

I better go. I have to do homework.

Love Always,
Katie

Katie made true to her promise. She wrote Aaron one letter every day as she promised Aaron she would. Katie wrote about soccer and school. She wrote about funny things that happened during the week. She wrote about it being cold outside and always asked questions to Aaron about how he was doing. Every once in a while, Katie would receive a letter from Aaron.

Katie,
I hope you are doing well. Things are different over here. Thank you for writing me. I just got back from a week out in the field. When I got back, I had all of your letters on my bed. It takes a while for the mail to get here, so when it does, I get all of them at one time.

This place makes me realize even more how much I love and miss you. When I get home, I am going to marry you.

I have to go; things are a little hectic around here. I will write you as soon as I can again.

Love,
Aaron

Katie finished reading Aaron's letter and set it down on her lap. *He wants to marry me.* Katie's heart was full, and she was so excited for the future. Sometimes Katie would get a phone call in the middle of the night.

The phone rang, and Katie's dad was woken after the third ring. "Hello?"

"Hey, Mr. George, I am sorry to wake you, but can I speak to Katie?"

"Yeah, hold on a minute." Katie's dad got out of bed and walked down the stairs to Katie's room. Katie's dad was also living the deployment. He would answer the phone each time Aaron called if Katie did not pick up. He would wake Katie up to talk to Aaron.

"Katie. Katie." Katie woke up and sat up in bed. It was her dad.

"What's wrong?" Katie looked over; it was three in the morning.

"Nothing. Aaron is on the phone." Katie's dad handed her the phone.

"Thank you."

Katie's dad while walking out of the room said, "Don't stay on too long."

Katie replied, "I wont."

"Aaron?" Katie said, trying to wake up.

"Hey, Katie," Aaron said.

"Are you okay? What's wrong?" Katie could hear and feel something was not right.

"I'm fine, Katie. Everything is fine. I miss you."

"I miss you too, Aaron. Are you sure you are okay?"

"Yeah, Katie, you don't have to worry about me."

"Are you counting down the days until you get to come home?"

"No, I would rather not think about it, to tell you the truth. I still have a long way to go."

"It will go by fast, and then you will be home, and we can spend lots of time together."

"Yeah, that would be nice, Katie."

"Aaron, are you sure you are alright?" Katie asked, worried. She just knew something wasn't right.

"Yeah, I'm just really tired."

Katie and Aaron talked for a few more minutes before Aaron said, "My time is up, Katie. I have to go."

"Okay, Aaron. I miss you."

"I miss you too, Katie. Hey, did I ever tell you I love you?"

"You did once or twice. Did I ever tell you I love you?"

Aaron grinned. "Yeah, once or twice."

"Bye, Katie."

"Bye, Aaron."

Katie rolled over, setting the phone next to her. She fell back asleep with an uneasy feeling that something was not right with Aaron. She just knew there was something Aaron was not telling her.

———◆— —◆———

Aaron hung up the phone and closed his eyes. He knew Katie knew something wasn't right. He did not want to worry Katie with the horrors he experienced the week prior. All the blood and all of the death would be too much. Aaron knew Katie was sheltered from the world, and he wanted to keep it that way. He did not want Katie to worry about him and the job he had to do. The job he signed up for, the job he was really good at doing. He needed Katie now more than ever, but he couldn't even tell her why. He couldn't explain how her letters were what kept him going, knowing when he came back in from the nightmares he was dealt, there was always a stack of letters waiting to be read. It was the only way he could be close to her at the time, and if that was all he could get, he would take it.

Katie and Aaron would continue to communicate while he was gone— Katie writing a letter every day, Aaron writing when he could and calling as much as he could. Despite the distance, the two stayed true to each other. The distance seemed to draw them closer together. When they couldn't speak, both somehow felt the ups and downs each was going through. When they felt it, Katie would write a letter to Aaron, encouraging him to keep going and she was waiting for him. Every time Aaron felt it, he would call to speak with Katie. The two were closer than either one of them could possibly understand.

Although they had a love that many will never experience in their lifetime, they were still kids. They had not experienced so much, and everyone but Aaron and Katie knew it.

That night, Katie sat down to write to Aaron.

> Aaron,
> I miss you. I have been thinking a lot about us. Why does everything have to be so hard? It is like everything is keeping us apart from one another. It shouldn't be like this. We should be together. It's just not fair. I don't know. I am just so confused. I know I love you with all of my heart. It is just so hard without you here.
>
> I love you,
> Katie

Katie was starting to have doubts. Everyone was telling her it was not going to work. She missed being close to someone. She missed having someone by her side. She felt alone and isolated from what people told her was the best years of her life. Katie felt she wasn't experiencing the things she needed to. But her heart told her to stay with Aaron, that he was the one for her.

With all the doubts floating around in Katie's head, it was felt by Aaron, and he knew he needed to call Katie.

"Hey, Ms. Sharon, can I speak with Katie?" Aaron said.

Katie's mom paused for a minute. "Aaron, you need to give Katie her high school years."

Aaron's heart dropped at Katie's mom's words.

"She needs to experience high school the way that you did. If you love her, let her have her high school years. Promise me you will."

Aaron was crushed. He knew that Katie was waiting on him. He knew that Katie was not experiencing things that she should. Aaron knew that Katie needed to grow, and he wanted her happy. Since Aaron left, Katie had not been herself, and he knew that. He knew that Katie yearned for him as much as he did for her. He needed Katie, and the fact that Katie's mom was telling him to leave her brought tears to his eyes.

"I love her, Ms. Sharon," Aaron finally said.

"I know you do, but if you love her, let her go for now. You can be together later when she gets out of school," Katie's mom explained.

He said, "I promise," and hung up the phone.

Katie heard the phone ring and walked upstairs to see who it was. When she reached her mom, her mom was hanging up the phone. The look on her face was one of sadness and hurt.

"Who was it, Mom?" Katie asked.

"Just Suzi from work," her mom stated.

"Oh, has Aaron called?"

"No, I haven't heard from him."

"Okay. Well, he is going to call soon. Just let me know," Katie said, walking away.

"I will, baby girl," Katie's mom said.

As Katie walked away, Sharon sat on the couch thinking about what she had just done. If Katie ever found out, Katie would be crushed. In Sharon's mind, it was the best decision she could have made for Katie. Katie had to grow up and experience new things. She was young, and Sharon did not want Katie to regret her high school years. Even though Sharon felt it was the best decision she could have made, her heart broke for Katie.

Aaron hung up the phone and laid back on the bed he called his own at the time. He began analyzing his decision, the positive and negative about it. Katie's mom was right; he knew Katie, and he trusted the love between the two of them. He did not want to let her go, but Aaron knew he had to. Aaron knew it was just a little bit longer before they would be together again. He made a promise to Katie's mom, and he promised himself he would let Katie go.

CHAPTER 7

"How long has it been?" Dylan asked.

Upset, Katie said, "Two months."

"What are you going to do?"

Katie angrily said, "Dylan, I don't know! I don't know what to do! He is my life, Dylan. It's not some fling like you have before moving to the next girl. It's real." After the words left Katie's mouth, she regretted every word she said.

Dylan was angered by Katie's response. "You got to let him go, Katie. He's not here. He has made the choice, Katie. He is living wherever the hell he is right now, and you are here. He's gone, Katie. It's time to live. What you had, yes, it probably was special, but it's over, and you are the only one that doesn't see it. I see it. Your other friends see it. Your parents see it. It was never going to work, and deep down you know that."

Dylan's words made Katie break down crying. Dylan hugged Katie. "You are going to be all right. We are going to get through this."

"I can't imagine not having him in my life."

"I know you can't, but maybe one day it will be different."

"Something is wrong. He wouldn't do this to me, Dylan," Katie said.

Dylan, pulling away, looked at Katie. "But he did."

When Katie got back home, she sat on the couch in deep thought. Dylan was right. Aaron had stopped calling and stopped writing through letters. Katie knew that something was wrong, that Aaron would not do that to her, but she could not figure out what happened. Katie did not know how to explain it, but she felt it. She felt in all of her heart Aaron was telling her to hold on.

Months went by that she did not hear from Aaron, but Katie kept her word to him. She continued to write him one letter a day as she promised him she would. Each letter would give a little bit of her life, but she never mentioned about his absence. She would talk to him like he was nothing more than a friend. Katie felt he needed that while he was over there doing what he was doing, which Katie had no clue because Aaron had kept the horrors he was experiencing to himself.

> Aaron,
> I hope you are doing well. It has been so busy this week. There was a dance at school this weekend, and it was alright. There was a bunch of us that went to eat and then to the dance. You know how school dances are; it was as good as they get. We went back to IHOP and hung out after. I think the waitress was ready for the loud bunch of us to leave. It was fun though. Next week some of us are going to go to the beach for the day; it will be fun. I better go for now. I just wanted you know I was thinking about you and to stay safe.
> Love Always,
> Katie

After each experience in the field, Aaron would return to the bed he called home. Each time, he would have a stack of letters from Katie. Each time, he would put them in order of the postmark date to read the story of what Katie was doing. He would read about things Katie was doing and experiencing; he would read about Katie going out with friends and living. He could tell that Katie was happy, and although his heart did ache for Katie, he knew at the time it was the best decision for her. At the end of each letter, Katie would write that she was thinking of him; and before signing her name, she would write, "Love Always." Aaron had faith that Katie still loved him, that Katie still wanted him in her life. So many times, Aaron thought about picking up the phone or writing a letter, but he didn't. He held on to the promise he made to Katie's mom months ago. All he had left was his word; he had lost Katie. Aaron needed Katie in his life. Maybe they could form a friendship one day. Aaron closed his eyes. *Wait for me*, he said in his head, hoping somehow Katie would hear him.

"How was the date with Daniel?" Dylan questioned as he and Katie ate in the food court at the mall.

"It was alright."

"Just alright?" Dylan questioned.

"He's not Aaron, Dylan," Katie said.

"Well, maybe he's not the one, but there are more fish in the sea," Dylan said, reassuring Katie.

"Yeah, I think I am doomed to be alone for the rest of my life," Katie said grumpily.

"At least you finally went out. It is a start."

"But I really don't want to go out with anyone, you know? All of them just aren't Aaron."

"Well, Katie, you have put Aaron on a pedestal and never lowered him down, even after he disappeared. He's not Prince Charming in the fairy tale in your head," Dylan said, smiling.

"I'm glad you think my love life is entertaining. How's Elaine?" Katie said, smiling.

"Mm, she's alright. She has issues," Dylan said, not amused, leaning back in his chair.

"Everyone has issues with you, Dylan."

"Well, I'm picky."

"Yes, you are."

The two were silent for a few minutes eating their lunch.

"Have you still not heard from him?" Dylan finally said, knowing Katie wanted to talk about it.

"No." She sat back in her chair, throwing her napkin on her plate.

"Are you still writing him every day?" Dylan questioned.

"Yes, one letter a day until he tells me he is home."

"Katie, how do you know he isn't home now? You could be writing him all these letters and he isn't even receiving them."

"I don't know how to explain it. I just know. I feel it. I know when he gets back, he will call me," Katie explained.

"No offense, but you know you are weird, right? You feel it?" Dylan said, laughing.

Katie smiled. "I know I sound weird, but it's a feeling."

Dylan and Katie picked up the food they were eating and threw it away in the trash can. Dylan and Katie hugged.

"Love ya," Dylan said to Katie.

"Love ya too," Katie said to Dylan as he walked away. "Hey, stay away from those crazies!" Katie yelled at Dylan. He waved, smiling as he walked away.

When Katie got home, she sat down at her desk and pulled out a piece of paper. Her thoughts were all of Aaron, and she daydreamed about the first time they met, the conversations they had together, and the kisses they shared together. She missed him more than he knew, and she wanted him to come back to her. She wanted him back so bad; she needed him.

Aaron,

Today I thought a lot about you and us
together. I miss you so much and I need
you, Aaron.

As Katie was writing those words, her dad appeared at the door. Katie turned around.

"Aaron's on the phone," Katie's dad said, holding the phone close to his chest. "Do you want to talk?"

Katie shook her head. "Yes."

Katie's heart dropped as her dad handed her the phone. As her dad walked away, she put the phone to her ear.

"Hello," Katie said as her heart was beating so fast, she thought Aaron could hear it.

"It's really good to hear your voice. I've missed you."

Katie closed her eyes. "I miss you too."

"I got back to the States last week."

"You did?"

"Yeah, I am going home for a few days to see my mom and then go to see my dad. Can I see you?" Aaron asked.

"Yeah, of course. When will you be here?" Katie asked.

"In about two days. I will call you once I get to my mom's house, if you want me to. Just to talk?"

Katie was in a daze that she was hearing Aaron's voice on the other end of the phone line. "Okay. That sounds like a plan."

"Okay, Katie, I know things have been hectic lately, but we are always friends, right?" Aaron asked.

Katie thought, *Friends, what the hell.* But she said, "Well yeah, duh."

Aaron laughed. "Okay, Katie, I will see you soon. Can't wait to see you."

"Me either, Aaron." Katie could not believe she was saying his name.

"Okay, well, I will see you then."

"Yeah," Katie said, not knowing what else to say.

Both paused, not knowing what else to say.

"Hey, Katie," Aaron finally said.

"Yeah."

"Did I ever tell you I love you?"

Katie's heart jumped at the words. "Yeah, once or twice. Did I ever tell you I love you?"

Aaron, happy with Katie's reply, said, "Yeah, once or twice. See you soon. Bye."

"Bye, Aaron."

Katie had been pacing her room but sat back down at her desk. She looked over at the letter she was writing Aaron.

> Aaron,
> Today I thought a lot about you and us
> together. I miss you so much and I need
> you, Aaron.

Katie picked up the letter, crumpled up the piece of paper, and threw it in the trash can. She picked up the picture of the two of them she had on her desk. She traced Aaron's face with her finger and whispered, "I love you," before setting the picture back down. Aaron was coming to see her, and he said he loved her. They were going to be alright.

CHAPTER 8

"He's coming home tomorrow to see his family and wants to see you?" Dylan said, rubbing his head.

Katie smiled. "Yes."

"Katie, I don't know what to say. I mean, he stopped talking to you for no reason, and then he just calls and says he wants to see you. Like you need to put everything on hold so you can see him."

The smile fell from Katie's face. "Yes, he told me he loved me."

"Yeah, Katie, but he has been MIA for months. Did you ask him what happened?"

"No, I didn't think about it. I was shocked he was on the phone," Katie explained.

"I just don't want to see you get hurt. I mean, you really don't know what he has been doing. He could have a girlfriend up there."

"I know, but we are friends." Katie tried to downplay Aaron's coming.

"Friends? Really? Friends with Aaron?" Dylan said with a surprised look on his face.

"Dylan, if we can't be together, I at least want him as a friend. I need that."

Dylan hugged Katie. "I just don't want you to get your hopes up."

"I won't, Dylan, I promise."

Katie knew the words she spoke to Dylan were a lie. Every emotion she felt for Aaron had resurfaced the minute she heard Aaron say, "Hey, Katie." It was the way he said her name. She couldn't wait to see Aaron; she was so excited that she could not sleep that night. She worried that it would not be the same. What if it was different? What if things had changed? What if he did not feel the same way he once did? Katie knew she had the same feelings, but what about Aaron? What if he was truly coming to see her as a friend? She fell asleep thinking about seeing Aaron for the first time in over a year.

The next day, each time the phone rang, Katie would answer it, hoping it was Aaron. Each time she was let down until finally:

"Hey, Katie, I'm on my way," Aaron said on the other line.

"Okay, I am here."

"See you in a few minutes. Bye," Aaron said.

"Okay, bye," Katie said before hanging up the phone.

Katie's heart started to pound; she started breathing hard. She jumped up and down. "Shit, shit, shit." Katie started taking deep breaths to calm down. She felt lightheaded. "Oh my god, oh my god, oh my god," Katie kept saying.

"So Aaron's coming, huh?" Katie turned; it was her little brother.

"Ryan, please not right now."

Ryan started laughing. "I'm headed to Brandon's house," Ryan said as he walked away, making kiss sounds.

Katie looked in the mirror. Would Aaron still find her attractive? Would he still like her? Would they still have a connection? It had been over a year since they saw each other. What would they talk about? Would they have the same things in common anymore? *Friends*, Katie kept telling herself. *He wants to be friends, Katie, nothing more.*

"Katie, Aaron just pulled up."

"Okay," Katie said, looking in the mirror one last time. Her heart was pounding, and she felt her stomach turning with butterflies.

She walked to the door and opened it. When Katie opened the door, Aaron had a few more steps before he met her. He smiled at Katie when he saw her. When he reached Katie, he picked her up, and they hugged each other for the first time in over a year. Katie closed her eyes, feeling every emotion in her body at once. She wanted to remember every second of the moment.

Aaron hugged Katie so tight. He did not want to let go of her. He had thought so many times about her while he was gone, and finally there she was. He didn't want to let her go. Aaron finally placed Katie back down. "I missed that."

"Me too," Katie said. She did not know why; but with one embrace from Aaron, every fear, every nervous thought just disappeared in seconds. He was her comfort, and she was his home.

The two walked back inside, into Katie's room, and sat down on the bed.

"Hi," Katie said, smiling.

"Hi," Aaron said, looking at Katie. Aaron pulled Katie's hair away from her face. Katie closed her eyes and placed her hand on top of Aaron's, resting his hand on her cheek.

"I've missed you so much, Aaron," Katie said, opening her eyes.

"I've missed you too, Katie, very much," Aaron admitted, pulling his hand away from Katie's face but keeping Katie's hand in his.

The two began to talk. Nothing had changed. They talked about everything that had happened in the past year, trying to catch each other up on their life since they were away from each other. It was like a year had not passed, like they picked up where they left off.

"So have you been out with other guys?" Aaron asked, wondering if Katie was seeing anyone else.

Katie knew the question would come up eventually, and she wasn't prepared to answer it at the time Aaron asked. She thought many times about not telling Aaron since he was coming home. She did not want to hurt him. To Katie's surprise, she said, "Yeah, once, not that big of a deal." Katie could not believe she was so honest with Aaron. She could tell by the look on Aaron's face it was not what he expected.

Aaron was taken aback by Katie's admission. She was living a life that Aaron was not a part of. Katie was moving past what they had or trying; he was hurt. He trusted Katie would wait for him, and everything in his body was telling him he was wrong about Katie. He never believed that Katie would ever see another guy the way she saw him.

As they talked, Aaron pulled his hand away from Katie's. They spoke for a short time more, and Aaron said, "I better go."

"You have to leave so soon?" Katie asked.

"Yeah, I have to drive down to my dad's house for a few days, but I will be back."

"Okay, will you come see me again when you get home?"

"Yeah, if I have time I will," Aaron said, getting up from the bed.

Katie walked Aaron to the door. Aaron walked out the door and started to walk away. He turned when he was a few feet away from Katie and looked at her. Katie looked at Aaron, and both did not say anything. Aaron turned back around and walked to his vehicle. Katie watched Aaron get into his car and watched him pull away until she could no longer see him.

Katie laid on her stomach with her head buried in the crease of her arm. She began to cry. That wasn't enough time to see Aaron. Katie knew he needed to spend time with his family, but it was unfair. *Why didn't he take me with him? I would have gone. We are just friends, that's why.*

In a few days, Katie received a phone call from Aaron.

"Hey, Katie, I'm sorry. I stayed at my dad's house longer than expected. I'm going to have to head back. I won't be able to see you before I go."

"It's okay. I understand," Katie said, disappointed.

"I'll see you next time I'm down."

"Okay, that sounds good," Katie said.

"Bye."

"Bye, Aaron."

Katie hung up the phone with Aaron and immediately called Dylan.

"He's gone."

"Already? I thought he was staying for a week?" Dylan questioned.

"Yeah, he went down to his dad's house and stayed longer than expected. He is going to head back."

"Oh, are you okay?" Dylan asked, not knowing what to say to Katie.

"Yeah, we are just friends. I am fine."

"Okay. I got to go, Katie. I am meeting Shelly."

"Who's Shelly?" Katie asked.

"Just a girl. I'll have to tell you later. Bye." Dylan hung up the phone.

Katie hung up the phone and went and sat at her desk. She picked up the picture of the two of them. Katie traced his face with her fingers. "I miss you," she whispered. She stared at it for a long time. To Katie, the picture symbolized a simpler time, a time with no confusion. In her heart, she knew that Aaron still loved her. Katie knew that she had a special place in Aaron's heart. In the back of her mind, Katie hoped for Aaron to come back just one more time. She dreamed of him coming back to surprise her, to hug her and tell her he loved her. Everything would be fine between them. Katie did not realize the impact of the few words she spoke: "Yeah, once." She had messed up.

CHAPTER 9

"It's our senior year, Katie. Can you believe it?" Dylan said excitedly.

"Yeah, finally. I am so ready to get out of school. I can't wait to be on my own and have a career," Katie said.

"You are the only person I know that wants to have a career but has no clue what that career is going to be," Dylan mocked Katie.

"Shut up. I will figure it out. I just haven't decided yet," Katie said, smiling at Dylan.

Katie had grown pretty independent since last seeing Aaron. She had dated some, but Katie got into the habit of dating people she could run all over. She would start dating them, and when they did one small thing that irritated Katie, she would move on to the next person. Katie could never make a decision on seeing someone for a long period. Katie was lost without Aaron and couldn't even see it.

"You will be married with five kids and stay at home," Dylan joked with Katie, knowing she would hate that life.

"Hell no, I'm not having kids or a husband. It isn't worth all the trouble." Katie smiled.

Katie had decided that kids were not for her. She couldn't imagine being married. She had no idea what she wanted to study in college or even if she wanted to go to college. Although Katie was so independent, she was lost. She was glad to be getting out of high school but did not know what the next chapters in her life would hold.

"What are you doing this weekend?" Dylan asked. "A bunch of us are going to Jeffery's graduation party. Do you want to come?"

"Hell no," Katie said, laughing. "Aaron is coming home next week. I think I am just going to stay at the house."

Dylan rolled his eyes. "Oh my god, you are still talking to him?"

"Yes, Dylan, we are friends."

"Friends?"

"Yes," Katie said, smiling.

"What are you guys going to do when he comes home?"

"I don't know, just talk probably."

"Just talk, that's it?"

Katie laughed. "Yes, Dylan, just talk."

"Right, sure, that's what you are going to do," Dylan said, mocking Katie.

Since Aaron left the last time, Katie and he gradually started talking most days for an hour at a time. Katie liked talking to Aaron even more these days as the normal surface-based conversations did not interest her anymore. She had grown up a lot since she saw Aaron last. Katie and Aaron passed it off as friends, but the two constantly flirted back and forth with each other over the phone. It was always more than "just friends." Of course, their conversation would stop eventually when Aaron would be overseas. But every once in a while, Aaron would call.

"So you're a senior now," Aaron joked with Katie.

"Why do you always give me a hard time?" Katie laughed at Aaron.

"Because I can, and the banter with you is fun."

"Well, Soldier Boy, when do you get back in town?"

"Ouch, I fly into North Dakota in the next week or so. I am going to get in the truck and start driving when we land."

"You're not going to be tired?" Katie asked.

"Well yes, Katie, but if I am going to see you before I go see my dad, I have to. My leave isn't that long this time."

"Ahh, you think you're a badass."

Aaron just laughed. "Something like that. It will be good to see you."

"Yeah, it's been way too long," Katie said with a smile.

"I will see you soon."

"Okay, Aaron, drive safe," Katie said.

"I will. Hey, Katie."

Without missing a beat, Katie said, "Did I ever tell you I love you?"

Aaron laughed. "Yes, once or twice."

Katie hung up the phone with a smile. Aaron always had a way of making her smile. He always made Katie feel full, that nothing was missing out of her life. When Katie was indecisive about a career in the future, Aaron was always there to comfort her. When Katie was having a bad day, she would always lean on Aaron to help her through it.

Aaron hung up the phone smiling as well. Katie always made his day better. The banter between him and Katie kept him alive. Knowing that he had Katie in his life, some part of it kept him from feeling so alone. Aaron, still deployed, took off his helmet and took out a crumpled picture. It was a picture of Katie that she had sent him a year earlier. He stared at it a long time, tracing her face with his fingers, speaking to Katie in his head. *When I get home, Katie, I am going to make it right, I promise. I am coming home for you.* Aaron folded the picture back up and placed it back in his helmet. He had carried it with him each deployment since he got it; it was his good-luck charm.

Just as he told Katie, Aaron got off the plane and dropped all of his stuff off and called her.

"I made it back," Aaron told Katie. "I'm on my way. I'll call you when I get closer."

"Okay, Aaron, drive safe."

Katie knew it was over a twenty-four-hour drive to get to her. It would not be until later/early morning hours a day away, before she would get to see him. But she was excited that she would see him soon. She knew they were only friends, but she still believed in them.

The next night, Katie was reading when Aaron called.

"Katie, I'm still pretty far away. I'm not going to get there until early in the morning."

"It's okay, Aaron. I will wait up for you. It's fine."

"I can't wait to see you," Aaron said, sounding exhausted.

"I can't wait to see you either, Aaron." Katie could hear how tired Aaron was through the phone.

Aaron was determined to fight through sleep to see Katie. Whenever he felt like dozing off, he would roll down his window and let the fresh air hit him in the face. He would play music, songs that reminded him of Katie; or in some instances, he would pull over and walk around just to wake himself up enough to continue the drive. The drive gave Aaron time to think as well. He thought about the first time he met Katie, the letters she sent him while being deployed, and her innocence. Katie had no understanding of the harsh realities of the rest of the world. Although Katie had not been his for a long time, he still believed in their relationship.

Around two in the morning, Katie saw headlights pull in the driveway. She quietly went to the door and opened it.

Katie whispered, "Hey, you." She could see pure exhaustion on Aaron's face, but he still smiled and said, "Hey, you."

They walked down the hall to the living room area.

"Can we just lie on the floor, Katie, and just talk?" Aaron said.

"Yeah, that is fine."

Katie grabbed some pillows and a blanket, and they laid on the floor. Aaron grabbed Katie and pulled her closer to him. "That's better. I miss this." Aaron kissed Katie's lips before pulling her even closer to him.

"Me too, Aaron," Katie replied. She placed her head on Aaron's chest. She could hear Aaron's heartbeat, and it was calming to her. Katie looked up at Aaron who had his head on her head. "I'm glad you are here."

Aaron, with his eyes closed, said, "I'm glad I'm here with you too."

Katie laid her head back on Aaron's chest and closed her eyes.

"Katie, Katie." Katie woke to Aaron calling her name.

She looked up at Aaron.

"Good morning," Aaron said, smiling at Katie.

Katie smiled back. "Good morning."

"I got to go, Katie."

Katie smiled and hugged Aaron. "But you just got here. I don't want you to leave."

Aaron rubbed Katie's back. "I don't want to leave, but I got to get down to my dad's house."

Katie groaned as Aaron sat up. Katie also sat up. "We really need to figure out what a bed is."

Aaron started laughing. "Yeah, probably."

The two sat and talked, laughing and reminiscing on past times between each other. They talked about their plans and where their life was headed.

"You know there has never been anyone that lived up to your standards," Katie said, smiling at Aaron.

"Oh really?" he asked, feeling thankful that Katie still considered him the one but sad for Katie not being loved the way she deserved.

"Yeah, really."

Katie and Aaron picked up where they left off. Time had not made things awkward; the emotions and the love were still there. They never had moments of nothing to say, but in the silence, it was comforting, and the two just knew everything was going to be okay. They didn't need to speak their feelings about each other; they both knew.

"Katie, I got to go," Aaron said after another hour had passed.

"I know. I am going to miss you. You're kind of addicting," Katie said, smiling.

Aaron laughed. He leaned over and kissed Katie's lips. "Can I call you later?"

"Of course," Katie said.

Aaron got up and stretched. "Errrr."

Both walked to the door.

"I need a hug," Aaron said, smiling at Katie.

Katie smiled and lifted her arms up. Aaron picked Katie up, and Katie threw her arms around Aaron's neck. "I miss you already," Katie whispered to Aaron. Aaron set Katie back down.

"I love you, Katie."

"I love you, Aaron."

He leaned down one more time and kissed Katie before walking away. As Aaron got into his truck, he looked over at Katie who was standing at the door. Katie blew Aaron a kiss and waved. She watched Aaron's truck go farther and farther down the road until she could no longer see it.

Katie walked back inside down the hallway to her room. She laid down on her bed and fell back asleep.

Katie got up later that afternoon and walked upstairs to her parents sitting at the kitchen table. She opened the refrigerator to get a glass of orange juice.

"Aaron didn't stay long," Katie's mom said.

"Yeah, he had to go to his dad's house today."

"Is he coming back to see you before he leaves?" Katie's mom asked.

"No, he doesn't have that much leave time. He is going to head back from his dad's house."

"You are okay with that?" Katie's mom questioned.

Katie, still a little groggy, did not have the energy to fight with her mom. "Mom, we are just friends. He can do what he wants to do." Katie closed the refrigerator and walked downstairs with the glass of orange juice.

As she was walking down the hallway, her eyes filled with tears. *No, I'm not okay with him not coming back, but there is nothing I can do about it.*

<hr>

Aaron, making it to his dad's house, was sitting around with family who had come by to see him. "How was the trip down here?"

"It was good, pretty smooth trip," Aaron replied.

"Did you have to stop?"

"No, I drove straight through," Aaron said. He did not want to answer any questions about Katie. He would rather not even mention her.

A day later, Aaron started the trip back to North Dakota. After making it back, he called Katie. "I made it back," he told her.

"That is good. I'm glad you made it safely," Katie said. She was a little angry. Not so much at Aaron but at life. Why did they never get any time together? Why did she feel they were cheated out of a life they could have together?

"You know, Katie, I was thinking, after you graduate, before you start classes, maybe you could come up here for a few weeks," Aaron said, hoping Katie would agree to it.

"Isn't it cold up there right now?" Katie asked.

Aaron laughed, knowing Katie hated the cold. "Yes, but I would keep you warm."

Katie laughed. "I will think about it."

"I would really like to show you around up here and where I live."

"Okay," Katie said, "I will think about it."

Katie had already made up her mind. She was going to North Dakota after she graduated. It would be summer and maybe a little warmer. She had decided on attending a technical college, and classes would not begin for a few months after she graduated. Katie had plenty of time to go see Aaron, stay with him longer than a day, and then come back. It would be perfect, and they could finally spend more than a couple of hours with each other. Katie was excited to see where he lived and meet his friends.

Katie and Aaron spoke often. Not every day, but when they did speak, they made plans for future events and seeing each other. Katie believed it was going to happen for them. It was what Katie wanted ever since the first day she met Aaron.

The closer to graduation it got, the more Katie and Aaron would speak. Katie had finished all of the requirements to graduate; she just had to attend classes until the last day of school. It gave her time to see all of her friends before they went different directions. Most were going to into the military and some going off to college. There were a few staying home like Katie. Only about a month away and she would be hugging Aaron. As Katie was thinking about it, the excitement was brewing inside of her. It was late, but she thought to herself, *Screw it, I am going to call Aaron.* Katie dialed Aaron's number.

"Hello," she heard Aaron say on the other end.

"Hey, I just want to talk to you," Katie said, smiling.

"Hold on a minute." She could hear shuffling.

Katie heard, "Who is it, Aaron? Aaron, who is it?" Katie's heart dropped; it was a female's voice on the other end of the phone.

Katie, in shock, said, "I'm sorry. I just wanted to talk."

"No, it's okay. Are you all right?" Aaron asked, concerned.

"Yeah, I'm fine. I just wanted to talk to you."

Katie could not shake what she had just heard. There was another woman at Aaron's house. Katie's world just came crashing down. She would not be going to North Dakota; she would not be seeing Aaron, and she had lost the only man she ever loved.

CHAPTER 10

It had been almost two years since graduation. Katie still did not know what she wanted to do for her career, so she had stopped going to school and was working two different jobs. She figured while she was figuring it out, she at least would be working, making money. She was still living at home but hoped to buy a house and move out from under her parents' house. Her mom had lightened up on Katie, but a curfew at twenty was not Katie's idea of fun. She was more than ready to become an adult.

Katie had not spoken with Aaron since the night she heard the woman's voice on the other end. Aaron must have figured it was over because he had not tried to call her either. The two had finally gone their separate ways. Katie half-heartedly told people it just wasn't meant to be. Katie's gut was telling her it wasn't the end, but her mind was made up. She was not going to keep dealing with the cycle of her and Aaron. She had to grow up and realize what they had was gone. Or at least that is what she was telling herself over and over again. She had to live in the now.

Katie was getting married. She had said yes to a man that she worked with. He was nice to her and did anything she asked of him. He was consistent, and he loved Katie with all of his heart. But Katie could never get to the point she did with Aaron. He never gave her the feeling of love and togetherness as Aaron did. Katie was lost, but with all the wedding planning, it was easy to get her mind off thinking if this was really what she wanted to do. It seemed like a production that she was planning, not a wedding. When she thought about marrying him, she became anxious; she would get nervous and shake. Katie kept telling herself everything was going to be fine, until it wasn't.

The phone rang, and Katie picked it up. "Hello."

"Hello," Katie repeated.

A voice she was all too familiar with was on the other line.

"Hey, Katie, how have you been?" It was Aaron. She had not spoken to Aaron in over two years. As soon as she heard his voice, every bit of what she had told herself to be true washed away. Every bit of emotion she had for Aaron came rushing back to her.

"Hey, Aaron, I am good. How have you been?" Katie said in shock.

"I haven't talked to you in a while, and I just wanted to see how you were doing."

"I'm doing good."

"Really?"

"Yeah, for the most part."

"That's not really convincing."

Katie started to laugh, something she had not done in a long time. "No, I'm good. I just wasn't expecting to hear from you."

"I hope it is okay to call. I just had a feeling that something was wrong, and I wanted to see if you were okay."

They always knew when something was going on with each other. It was one of those things they both could not explain, but they felt it. The two began to catch up on the last two years that had passed. Aaron talked about being deployed a lot, and Katie talked about working two jobs to figure out what she wanted to do. Neither one mentioned the last time they spoke. It was like anything in the past had been wiped away by the two talking.

"Hey, I am coming home soon. Do you think I could see you?"

"Yeah, of course," Katie said without knowing how she was going to explain it to her fiancé.

"Are you dating anyone, Katie?"

Crap, Katie didn't want to answer that question. "Yeah, umm, Aaron, I am getting married." A short pause ensued.

"Wow, Katie, that is great."

"Yeah," she said, not convincing Aaron it was what she really wanted to do.

"Do you love him, Katie?"

"He is not you if that is what you are asking," Katie continued. "He loves me, and he is here, and I bought a house."

"When are you getting married?"

"March 16 at the Serenity House," Katie replied.

"That is coming up fast. Congratulations, Katie."

Aaron could not believe what he was hearing. He was too late. Katie was getting married, and there was nothing he could do. She had found someone else to love and share her life with. Aaron's mind was spinning, and all he could think of was all the decisions he had made that brought the two of them to the current situation.

He didn't understand that it was Katie's decisions that had put them in the predicament they were in. Katie wanted to get out of the house from under her mother and was trying to search everywhere to find Aaron in everyone she dated. When she couldn't find him, she decided to settle for someone who she knew loved her. Katie thought she could live with the decision she was making. Well, until she picked up the phone and heard Aaron's voice on the other end. In a matter of seconds, Aaron had brought back so much emotion and all the love she had for him. She knew she was making the wrong choice, but there was nothing she could do; she already said yes to another guy.

"So tell me about this house. That is exciting, your first house."

"Yeah, there was a lady that just got married, and she wanted to get rid of her house, so she sold it to me for what she owed on it. It worked out pretty well."

"Have you already moved in?"

"No, that is a long story. My mom didn't want me to move out until I got married."

"I see Sharon is still making decisions for you," Aaron said.

"Yes, she is, part of the reason I am ready to get out of the house."

"Well, I will let you go, Katie. I will call you when I make it down that way, and we will meet and catch up."

"Sounds good, Aaron. It was really good to talk to you."

"It was good to talk to you, Katie."

Katie hung up the phone and sat down with her thoughts. What was she doing? She couldn't do this; she couldn't get married. It was a sign. Why would Aaron call out of the blue and talk to her if it wasn't a sign? The life Katie was planning all of a sudden didn't fit with what she wanted.

Katie never heard from Aaron on his trip home. She figured it was because of the bombshell she threw at him. Katie believed she would never hear from Aaron again. She decided to proceed with the choices she had made, which meant getting married to someone who wasn't Aaron.

———————————

"Hey, darling, are you okay?" Katie's fiancé was standing next to her for rehearsal. Katie was getting married to the man standing next to her tomorrow.

"Yeah, I am fine. Just a lot on my mind."

"Tomorrow is going to be perfect, Katie. You have done a great job planning with your mom."

"Thanks." Katie already hated the way he said her name.

The pastor said, "You will turn toward each other. We will say the vows you have prepared. After that, I will say a prayer, and you will turn and face the congregation, and I will pronounce you husband and wife. And that is it."

Katie smirked at the pastor and her fiancé. She was so done with all of it; she just wanted to hurry and get it over with. Her fiancé kissed her cheek and smiled at her. Katie smiled back at him half-heartedly. All she could do was think about Aaron. *This should be Aaron, not him. I should be marrying Aaron, not this guy.* Katie felt like a fraud. She felt like she was lying to everyone she knew who would witness her marrying her fiancé tomorrow. She couldn't back out of it now. Her parents had paid so much money for the wedding. There were family members from all over the United States here to witness Katie get married. All Katie could think was *What have I gotten myself into?*

The next day, Katie was waiting in the bridal suite. She was striking, standing in her off-the-shoulder wedding dress. Her hair was pulled back, and she wore a tiara. A veil fell across her face and down her back, reaching the floor. Several people had come and congratulated her, told her she looked beautiful, and were so happy for her. Katie was standing in the room with her elder brother. Her mind was spinning. Her anxiety was working overtime, and she tried to act calm in front of her brother as everyone came and went from the room. Katie looked in the mirror and could only think of Aaron. She secretly hoped that Aaron would walk through the door and tell her not to marry her fiancé. She hoped Aaron would come and tell her to marry him and to be with him for the rest of her life. She kept looking toward the door, but Aaron never walked in. She wished Aaron would save her from what she was about to do.

Katie was lost in her thoughts when Dylan walked in. "Katie, you look beautiful."

"Thanks, Dylan."

Looking at Katie, Dylan said, "Are you ready for this?"

Katie looked at Dylan, and he knew she wasn't ready. "You are going to be fine. I will see you outside." He kissed Katie on the cheek and walked out.

The music started playing in the church. Katie looked toward the door it was coming from. Katie's elder brother was watching Katie and her reactions.

"You know, Katie, if you don't want to do this, you can take my car and go. We will tell everyone, and I'll deal with Mom."

Katie's dad walked in the room and said, "Are you ready to go?"

Katie thought about what her elder brother said. Her lip had started to quiver. She stretched her neck to the left and right and took a deep breath. "No, let's do this." Katie grabbed her dad's arm, and they went out to walk down the aisle.

Katie was in a daze, and she bit her lip trying to get her lip to stop quivering.

"Repeat after me: 'All that I am, and all that I have, I give to you.'"

Katie thought about the vows she was making. *"All that I am, and all that I have, I give to you." What does that actually mean?* She had not given the best to her fiancé as she had given to Aaron. She felt her life was a fraud and was still hoping that Aaron would come rushing through the door, but he did not. There was nothing Aaron could do for her; she had done this to herself.

"I now pronounce you husband and wife. You may kiss the bride." Katie half smiled and kissed her now husband, pulling away as soon as their lips touched. She had married a man who wasn't Aaron, and that was it. She would never marry Aaron or be with Aaron again. She had made the worst mistake; she did not want to be married.

"You did it, Katie." Dylan smiled.

"Yeah, I did."

"I got to head out. Sorry I can't stay, but we are going to drive up tonight so when I leave tomorrow, it won't be too early." Dylan was leaving for boot camp. After being out of high school and realizing college wasn't for him, he joined the Marines.

"I will miss you," Katie told Dylan, giving him a hug.

"You're a married woman now. You won't have time for me," Dylan said, laughing.

"Call me when you can, okay?"

"I will. Bye, Katie," Dylan said, kissing her cheek.

"Bye." Katie watched Dylan walk away. He was excited, but Katie's heart ached. She would miss Dylan. He was the only one left in Georgia she trusted with her secrets, with her thoughts of Aaron. Dylan knew her for who she was, just like Aaron did, and now both were gone.

Katie walked into her reception feeling alone. She spoke with everyone at the reception. They cut the cake, people toasted to the newly married couple, and everyone had a grand time. Katie and her now husband left for their honeymoon. Her husband was so excited being married to Katie, and he tried to please Katie in every way he could imagine. He could tell that Katie was irritated; but he thought it was because of the early morning, all of the people, and the stress of everything being perfect. In all reality, Katie was just hoping she could settle into her new life with her now husband.

The honeymoon was about as stressful as the wedding for Katie. Mudslides caused roads to wash out. The cabin they rented was built on a steep incline, so steep Katie refused to stay in it, and the two had to rent a hotel room. Katie knew all of this was a sign; this marriage wasn't right. Needless to say, when they got home, they settled into the house that Katie bought. They got into a routine of how life was going to be; they even had a new puppy. Seven months later, Katie could not take it anymore. She called her parents and told them she was getting a divorce; she could not do it any longer.

To say her husband was upset would be an understatement. It was not a good situation at all. Anger overtook him, and the day he was moving out, Katie left and went to her parents' house. When Katie made it home that evening, she found that the house had been trashed. Her clothing was thrown all over the floor. Dishes were all over the counters. In the living room, movies and other items that were once in a cabinet were thrown on the floor. It truly looked like someone had burglarized her house. Katie just took a deep breath and started to pick up and put away all of the items around the house. Out of everything that just happened, it was not that big of a deal. Tomorrow, she had scheduled for her locks to be changed, and she would be safe. Katie would never have to see him or hear from him again.

Ten months after the wedding, three months after the separation and divorce, Katie received a phone call. "Hey, Katie," it was Aaron. She had not spoken to Aaron since the day she told him she was getting married.

"Hey, Aaron, how are you doing?"

"I am good. How is married life?" Aaron asked.

"I'm divorced."

Aaron's heart dropped. *Katie is divorced from her husband.* "I'm sorry, Katie. Are you okay?"

Katie took a deep breath. "Yes, I am okay."

Chapter 11

To say Katie's mom was pissed was an understatement. She spent a lot of money on the wedding that Katie wanted for it to last seven months. Katie's mom was embarrassed, and you could hear the disgust in her voice every time Katie talked to her. But one of the good things about it was that Katie was out of the house and could come and go as she pleased. She paid her own bills; no one was going to tell her what she could or could not do. She only had to deal with her mom on Sundays when she would go over to the house for dinner. To help with the bills, Katie got a roommate. It was one of her childhood friends Sarah, from Florida, who thought she wanted a change of scenery and moved to Georgia. It was working so far.

Katie and Sarah would go out almost every night. To say they were living it up in their twenties was an understatement. Each night they would show up at their favorite pub to drink and dance the night away. They would get home around three each morning and crash. Katie would sleep for a few hours and get up to head to work, as she was the manager who would open early. She would rather be the closing manager, but that would always put her rushing home to get ready to go out with Sarah.

Men in Katie's life were far and in between. She had sworn off guys and would never settle down with one. She talked to guys online, a new thing termed "social media." She wasn't ready to settle down again. Since the marriage and the subsequent divorce, Aaron and Katie had talked on and off. They had become friends and nothing more since the divorce. Katie just enjoyed talking to Aaron, as they both talked about the crazy times they were having. It was good to have Aaron in her life again. He made her happy, and she felt loved and safe. Since Dylan was gone, Katie confided a lot in Aaron again. She always talked to Dylan about what she was feeling, but with Dylan gone, Aaron became her rock.

Aaron had been overseas several times. It had become just a natural thing. Since the internet's birth, it was a little easier to keep in contact with Aaron.

"Hey, you," Aaron said when Katie picked up the phone.

"What are you doing, Aaron?"

"I am coming home for the weekend. Do you want to hang out?"

"Yeah, of course. Where are you going to stay?"

"I was thinking at my mom's house. Not sure yet."

"Why don't you stay at my house? It's just me and Sarah here. You can sleep in my bed or on the couch."

"Are you trying to tell me something, Katie?" Aaron teased.

Katie started laughing. "I'm being nice. Remember, you're not going to get in my pants."

Aaron laughed, remembering when Katie told him the exact same thing when they were in high school. "I will think about it."

"Okay, just figured I would offer," Katie said. "When are you coming?"

"I'll be in town Friday sometime."

"Okay, sounds good."

Katie was excited. She had not seen Aaron since they had fallen asleep on the floor years earlier at her parents' house. Although Aaron and Katie had been friends for a few years now, Katie still hoped that one day they would be a couple again. She hoped that somehow, they could make it work again. As time had passed and they were in their twenties, things had not changed between the two. They still had a bond that Katie never had with anyone else. They never ran out of things to say, and they had a connection so deep, each could feel what the person was thinking. As time had passed, they began to understand each other more. Instead of time pulling them apart as it does with a lot of people, it seemed to pull them together.

———————————•—•   •—•———————————

"Katie, you will never believe what I am looking at out my back door," Dylan said.

"What?" Katie wondered.

"Kangaroos, there are tons of them." Dylan was stationed in Australia and was loving every minute of it.

"Awww, go pet them," Katie said.

"Hell no, they will kick your ass," Dylan said.

"I talked to him," Katie said.

"Mmm really, what did he say?" Dylan asked, not amused. He knew exactly who she was talking about. Katie didn't even need to say his name.

"He's coming here on Friday to see me."

"Katie, you need to just leave it alone," Dylan said, sounding irritated.

"We are just friends. We are just going to see each other."

"Right, just friends."

Katie giggled. "Yes, Dylan, just a friend."

"Just be careful, Katie."

"Yes, Dad, I will be careful," Katie said, mocking Dylan.

"It's never going to end, is it?"

"Well, I hope not. We are friends."

"Katie, the two of you can never just be friends. You know that," Dylan said. "I got to go, Katie. Please be careful."

"I will, Dylan."

On Friday, Aaron arrived as he said he would. As usual, the two talked for hours on end. They never ran out of things to talk about.

"Hey, you want to lie on the floor for old times' sake?" Katie asked Aaron.

The two laid on the floor and continued talking. And talking was what they did while they cuddled up next to each other. Sarah would hear the two talking and laughing. She let them be as she thought the whole dynamic of the two was in other words different. Sarah did not understand how the two proclaimed their love for each other, spent hours talking and cuddling with each other, but never once had been intimate. Katie would always tell Sarah it was more than just sex.

"I have to work tomorrow early, but I figured I would be home about the time you are getting up. And we can spend the rest of the day together."

Aaron kissed Katie's forehead. "That sounds perfect."

The night for Katie was perfect. She and Aaron got to catch up, and they were going to sleep in the same bed together, like adults. Of course they shared many kisses between them. The next day, she would get up and go to work and come home to Aaron. It was a mini version of what Katie wanted.

When Katie returned home, she noticed Aaron's vehicle was gone. She tried to call Aaron, but he did not answer the phone. When she walked inside, Sarah was watching TV.

"Where's Aaron?" Katie asked Sarah.

"He said he had to go and that he would call you later," Sarah said.

"Did he say where he was going?" Katie questioned.

"No," Sarah said, continuing to watch TV.

Katie went to her room and sat down at her makeup table. Something wasn't right. Why did Aaron leave? They were supposed to spend another day and night together.

Aaron finally called in the evening time. "Hey, Katie."

"What happened, Aaron? Why did you leave?" Katie asked.

"I had to leave. I couldn't stay there," Aaron said.

"Did Sarah say or do something?"

"No, she didn't."

Katie wondered what she had done. Why did he have to leave so suddenly? Why did he seem that he was blowing off the day and night that they spent together? Katie did not understand what happened. She thought everything was fine when she went to work.

Aaron was gone, and he and Katie did not speak for months. Since the last time she and Aaron had spoken, Katie had managed to kick Sarah out and was living on her own. She worked, went to school, and came home completely exhausted, trying to make ends meet. Katie was making it on her own, and for the first time in a while, she enjoyed the peace of her own company. As expected though, it did not take long before she and Aaron were speaking again. No matter what either did to the other, they could not stay away from each other. Each time they would be pulled apart, something always pulled them back together. It was like a sick joke; they would get a taste of each other's presence, but then life would pull them apart. Katie became immune to the friendship and chemistry between them; she knew they would see each other, not talk for a while, and then start talking every day again. It was a cycle the two always followed, which always led back to them being together.

"Katie, I am going to be down for a few days in Florida. You want to meet up and talk?"

"Yeah, what day? I am off on Wednesday and Friday."

"How about Wednesday?"

"Okay, just send me the address and I'll find it."

Katie drove to the location that Aaron had told her about. She knew of the land as Aaron had talked about it before with her. She pulled off the road and followed the trail back into the woods until she couldn't see the road. She saw a cabin and Aaron standing on the front porch.

"Secluded much?" Katie asked Aaron jokingly.

"It's peaceful," Aaron said, smiling.

The two walked inside, and Katie began looking around. It was a small cabin, and it looked like Aaron was working on it.

"I'm fixing it up. It's not big, but it works for getting away and hunting," Aaron explained.

Katie groaned and joked, "Animal killer." She had been a vegetarian since high school. Aaron just smiled, knowing Katie's views on hunting.

The cabin was small with little space to sit, so Aaron and Katie sat on the bed and talked.

"What is it like over there?"

"What, overseas?" Aaron asked.

"Yeah?" Katie asked.

"It's just different, Katie. The people are just evil."

"Well, I am sure they are alright, but they just . . ." Katie could not finish her sentence before Aaron said, "They are all evil, Katie."

Katie got quiet, and Aaron said, "I'm sorry, Katie. You just don't understand those people like I do. They are really bad people."

"It's okay, Aaron."

"So how is work?" Aaron asked, changing the subject.

"It is alright. I've realized that there is no way I want to do this type of job forever. I started going back to school. I really don't know what I want to do, but I figured I have a few years before I have to decide."

Katie continued, "I thought by now I would have figured out what I wanted to do, but I still just don't know. I'm supposed to decide what I want to do for the rest of my life, and I am finding it hard to decide on one thing."

Aaron smiled, looking at Katie talk. He could feel her frustration talking about a career she still had no clue on. He took his hand and pulled her hair away from her face. "You will figure it out," he said.

"Yeah," Katie said, not convinced.

"I've missed you," Aaron said, looking at Katie.

"I've missed you too," Katie said.

Katie smiled at Aaron and leaned over and hugged him.

Aaron rubbed Katie's back. "That's better."

Aaron and Katie pulled back but still were face-to-face. Aaron moved forward and kissed Katie. All the emotions the two felt for each other came pouring out, as if they had not seen each other in years. All of the love heightened with each kiss and each touch of the other's skin. Aaron laid Katie back on the bed. He began to kiss Katie's neck, and Katie ran her fingers down Aaron's back. She started to breathe heavy and shake.

"I'm shaking," Katie finally said.

"Are you sure you want to do this?" Aaron asked.

Katie looked into Aaron's eyes. "Yes."

Aaron and Katie interlocked their hands together and were intimate for the first time.

CHAPTER 12

"You slept with him?" Dylan said, puzzled.

"Yeah," Katie said, laughing.

"I thought you guys were just friends?" Dylan said.

"We are friends, I think. I don't know, Dylan," Katie tried to explain to Dylan while her mind continued to spin since the incident.

"And you haven't heard from him?"

Katie said no.

"Katie, I think you need to realize it is not like it once was. The Aaron you knew is different now. Yes, it may have been special. Yes, he may have been the one for you at one time, but it's different now. Katie, we are adults, doing adult things. You have to let what you think the two of you still have go. Obviously, Aaron doesn't think of it the same way."

"It just hurts, Dylan. He feels like home to me." Katie began to tear up.

"Katie, that is not what you are getting through your thick head. There is no home, Katie. You guys aren't together. Jesus Christ, Katie, think about it!"

"I love him, Dylan!" Katie exclaimed.

"Katie, I know you do, but what the hell. He isn't even around half the time. What now, every time he is in town he will just stop by?" Dylan was mad. Katie could hear it in his voice.

"It's not like that, Dylan."

"Katie, it is, girl. You two are not together. You haven't been for years. Just let it go, Katie."

"He contacts me, Dylan. I don't call him."

Dylan replied, "That doesn't mean anything, Katie. He knows you will pick up the phone."

"I got to go, Dylan." Katie did not want to talk anymore. She did not want to hear what Dylan was saying any longer.

Katie hung up on Dylan. He was right; she and Aaron were nothing more than friends for years now. He had not mentioned about the two of them being an item in years. They were at best friends, now with benefits. Aaron wouldn't use her though; it wasn't like that between them. It was more, even if they did not say they were an item, they both meant more to each other. What happened meant something to both of them.

Katie again had not called Aaron, and Aaron had not called her. She managed to find other guys that she could run all over but were crazy about her. She would date each of them until she got tired of them or found someone else, then she would leave them.

Katie liked guys that she could control. She liked being in charge, and she liked knowing that no matter what, they would always be with her, and the only way they would leave is if Katie left them. It was a comfort for Katie. The control of her own fate being in her own hands was what Katie needed. She did not care if anyone liked it; she was not going to give up control of what went on in her life anymore. Katie was done searching for a fairy tale; there was no such thing.

As predicted by Katie, Aaron called after about a year, to check up on her. This time, Katie was closed off to Aaron.

"Hey, Katie," Aaron said, chipper.

"Hey, Aaron, how are you?" Katie said, sounding not amused.

"Are you okay?" Aaron asked, puzzled.

"Yeah, I'm good, just been busy," Katie said.

"What have you been up to?" Aaron asked, trying to ignore the disconnect between them.

"Nothing much. I went into law enforcement. I am policing in town. Been doing it about six months now."

Aaron was shocked. "Law enforcement, Katie?" Aaron could not believe of all things, Katie went into law enforcement—a career that was full of evil in the world and where she could get hurt at any time.

"Yeah, I started taking criminal justice class as an elective in college and liked it, so I applied and got hired," Katie replied.

"Well, congratulations on finding the career you always wanted."

"What have you been up to?" Katie sounded uninterested, but she longed to know what Aaron was doing. She missed him and missed talking to him.

"I'm just working."

"Are you still in the military?"

"For now, I am going to get my degree and see where that leads me."

"Well, that is good. You married or dating anyone?" Katie tried to sound uninterested, but she was curious to know if Aaron had found anyone. Just talking to him, Katie wanted to be closer to him.

"No neither. Katie, I know things were off last time, but can we see each other? Just as friends, just to talk?"

Katie knew she should not meet Aaron. She knew all the emotions and all the passion they shared with each other would come back. She knew it would go back to the same unknowing and confusion of what they were. She knew she should tell Aaron no, that she didn't think it was a good idea; but instead, she said, "Yeah sure. When do you want to meet?" They were just friends. She was not going to let Aaron get close to her heart.

"How about during the week next week? What days are you off?"

"Tuesday, Wednesday, and Thursday," Katie said. It would be perfect through the week.

"Let's do Thursday. Is that okay?"

"Yeah, that is fine. I will leave early in the morning and head your way. Just send me the address. Where are you staying?"

"Okay, I will do that."

"Oh okay. Well, I will see you then?"

On Thursday, Katie drove to the address that Aaron had given her. She knocked on the door, and Aaron answered it. He smiled and picked her up, hugging her. There was always a comfort both of them felt just by a hug. In those moments, both felt safe, and any fear each of them had about seeing each other dissipated.

Katie and Aaron did what they always did. They talked and caught up with each other. They laughed about what silly things they had done. They told each other their secrets, the things they were proud of, and their dreams. They would talk about the dark sides of their jobs that no one but the few understood. Aaron and Katie both knew their secrets were safe with each other. Always the first part of their meeting was friendly banter, joking, and secret telling. But as the day progressed, the two could not help the feelings that would arise in their hearts. Being in the same room together would send every emotion spinning. Every stare and every glance had both of them falling in love with each other all over again. It brought back the truth of what the two already knew—they were meant for each other. There was no time, no distance that would ever keep them apart. The chemistry and the passion between Katie and Aaron were too much. Aaron and Katie would lean into each other at always the right time, and the passion came out with each kiss they shared.

Katie and Aaron knew if they had the chance to see each other, neither would deny the encounter. Ten years later, they both were very stubborn and fought it. Maybe because they were young, maybe not, but life always would pull them back toward each other. Both knew with each goodbye, it wasn't forever; they would always find each other again.

Katie and Aaron spent the day, Thursday, with each other. It was a perfect day filled with the special love they had for each other. History repeating itself, the two did not speak for a few months after. The only conclusion Katie could come up with was that the chemistry between the two of them was too much, and one or the other could not handle it. That is why they would always walk away. Katie was content with that reasoning and would always throw herself into work.

Katie loved working in law enforcement. The job gave her an adrenaline rush each time something exciting came out. She was used to seeing bodies and used to fighting individuals who were trying to escape from getting arrested. She became numb to the language of those she was arresting or the names she would be called on a daily basis. Katie had fit in easily in the male-dominated field due to her many years of being "one of the guys."

Katie continued to rise in the department she was working for. She had the respect of the other officers and was really good at her job. Others loved working with her because they knew, no matter what, Katie would stay in the fight. They could trust in her and her abilities.

Katie and Aaron continued to email mostly. Sometimes they would message each other as cell phones became more accessible. Aaron and Katie had fallen into a friendship, a true friendship. They had not spoken about their past; they just moved forward in the future as friends. Each of them wanted the other in their life, and they both knew a friendship was the only way to ensure that.

> Aaron,
> I was thinking about you today. You would not believe the stuff I saw yesterday at work. I am about to go to a different unit. I'm excited. It will be so much fun. I will be working overnight, but the hours are pretty good. You know right before you get tired, you get off. I hope you are doing well. Are you gone? If so, come home safe.
>
> Love Always,
> Katie

Katie,
I am happy for you, Katie. Yes, I am deployed again. It seems like I am always sleeping everywhere but my own bed. I have been thinking about you too and wondering how you have been doing.
When I get home, do you want to maybe meet up and grab coffee?

Love,
Aaron

Aaron,
You are always gone. :) I don't know how you do it. Yes, I think that would be great. Yesterday at work, you won't believe what happened. My partner and I got in a chase, and we had to tackle this guy, and he was fighting us. So crazy how people will fight the police. I didn't know people were like that. Just weird to see and be involved in.
I hope you are doing well and staying safe.

Love Always,
Katie

Katie had gained a bigger, bolder personality. She was around a bunch of police officers who thought that laughter kept the stresses of the job at bay. Laughter would always make whatever was going on easier to deal with.

Katie finally had the career that she wanted, and she was good at it. She was soon moved to a specialized unit and loved the people she worked with. They became her family as they were the only ones who knew exactly what she went through on a daily basis. She began distancing herself from the friends she once had, as they did not understand what she was going through. On nights she wasn't working, several would go out drinking, to just have fun and forget what they had endured the week before.

Katie's view on the world began to change. The fairy tale Katie once thought was the world was actually a dark, evil place. She saw everyone as a threat, and she saw everyone around her besides the people she worked with as evil. All but her immediate family and Aaron.

Katie thought often of what Aaron must see on a daily basis when he was deployed. She realized how sheltered she was from the world and that Aaron, knowing years before she did, never once told her different. He allowed Katie to live in her bubble and the fairy tale that she called life. She wondered if, at times when she called talking nonsense, Aaron had just endured the evil she had become so aware of. Suddenly, her own life did not seem that important to tell Aaron.

Her heart ached for Aaron, knowing he had seen worse than she had. Katie couldn't imagine the horrors he lived while being deployed. She would email Aaron when she thought about what he could possibly be facing.

One day, Aaron called Katie frantic, catching Katie off guard because he was actually home.

"Katie, my brother is going to prison."

"Aaron, what is going on?"

Aaron began telling Katie the story of his brother and the horror he was living. How he was hurt and embarrassed. Katie listened intently as she had experienced the same shock years earlier as a teenager.

"Aaron, it's going to be okay. You know I get it. You did nothing wrong, sweetheart. You did the right thing. Is there anything I can do?"

"No, I just needed to talk to you."

"I'm here always for you, Aaron."

The conversation was over almost as soon as it started. Katie had never heard Aaron like that before. She could tell he had every emotion dealing with the situation. Katie felt horrible for him but did not want to pry. Katie remembered not wanting to talk about it at the time. Katie figured Aaron would talk about it when he wanted to, but she would make sure Aaron knew she was there for him.

> Aaron,
> I just wanted to let you know I was thinking about you. I hope you are being safe. Know that someone back home loves you very much.
>
> Love Always,
> Katie

In their late twenties, the emails continued between Aaron and Katie. Katie would encourage Aaron, making sure to tell him she was thinking of him and loved him; and Aaron would send his love to Katie, wanting to see her again. They were friends, but it felt as if the space between them wasn't as far as it actually was. They could feel each other through the emails, an indescribable phenomenon both had grown to accept. Pain, love, or happiness, it would depend on which came through the email; but all were felt in each other's heart. They may not have each other, but they had a bond of some kind, and both enjoyed the safety in their bond.

> Katie,
> Guess what, I am coming home soon.
> You want to grab that cup of coffee?
> Love,
> Aaron
>
> Aaron,
> Yeah, that will be awesome to see you after all this time. Just let me know when you are back, and I will see you then. I am thinking about you and miss you.
>
> Love Always,
> Katie

Katie had come to the conclusion that she and Aaron were never going to be more than friends. She thought it was fate that kept pulling them apart. She had made a lot of dumb mistakes, and she knew Aaron would always forgive her for them, but it was a thorn that was not so easy to pull out of Aaron's side. They had settled into friendship. Not seeing each other and the distance between them made it easier for Katie to realize their life together was nonexistent.

Katie continued to date. She would like to believe that she was dating people to find someone that she got along well with and gave her the feeling Aaron did. She always looked for Aaron within them though. The only thing she dared not to do was date anyone much taller than her. It was one of those secret things, one of those things she would never do. In a way, Katie thought that was her way of not trying to find Aaron in another guy; it was her justification that she was "over" Aaron.

As the phone rang, Katie looked down to see it was Aaron calling. Katie's stomach dropped; she did not understand why. It was just Aaron. Why was she nervous to pick up the phone?

"Hey, Katie," Aaron said, chipper.

"Aaron, it's good to hear from you. How are you doing?" Katie said, trying to sound just as chipper.

"I'm doing good. I have some big news," Aaron said.

"Whatcha got, Aaron? Hit me with it," Katie joked.

"I'm getting married," Aaron said excitedly.

Katie's heart dropped. She sat down in the chair that was next to her. Shocked, she said, "Oh wow, that's great, Aaron. Congratulations. I'm so happy for you."

"Thanks. I am excited. I did it right, got the big ring . . ." Aaron continued to tell Katie how he proposed, how they met, and the sequence of events leading up to them getting engaged.

"Katie?" Aaron asked at Katie's silence. She had been silent, and her thoughts were going so fast that she didn't even think to say something to Aaron.

"Yeah, I am here. That is awesome. I am so happy for you, Aaron. You deserve to be happy," Katie said.

"Well, I got to go, Katie. I have more people to call, but I wanted you to know. You are one of my oldest friends," Aaron said. The words were a dagger to Katie's heart.

"Of course, Aaron. Again, congratulations!" Katie said, acting excited.

Katie hung up the phone and sat with her thoughts. *Aaron replaced me.* That was so hard for Katie to believe. She thought Aaron would always be single and that she was the one who was the drifter. Katie always thought she could drift back to Aaron, and he would always be there, but now, he was going to have a wife. Someone he had to give all of his time to, and she would be that "friend" that Aaron always told people they were. It was more to Katie than just friend though. It was always more. Katie was crushed. She knew it was her burden to carry; she was the one who pushed Aaron away and, well, got married.

Instead of letting it go, Katie would take out all of her frustrations at work. Everyone blew it off as Katie becoming jaded to the world because of law enforcement. In the world of law enforcement, evil is the only thing you see. Katie kept her thoughts to herself and continued on. She was starting to believe that the only person she could count on was herself. It was up to her to make her life exactly what she wanted, and she continued to push to do more and be more in life.

Katie and Aaron were still friends. They would talk on occasion and catch up on married life and their jobs. Katie knew she was replaced and did not want to cause Aaron problems. She put every bit of feelings away and became only a friend to Aaron, one thing she never believed she could be. Katie's mind told her to hang on. In some way, they would still end up together. Katie began to think she was crazy. Then there was another phone call from Aaron she wasn't expecting.

"Katie, guess what?"

"What is it, Aaron? You are happy today," Katie said, amused.

"I'm going to be a dad," Aaron said. Katie could tell she was on speakerphone.

"Oh my gosh, I'm so happy for you. Kids are awesome," Katie said without pausing.

Katie could hear Aaron talking to his wife in the background.

"Are you both excited? Do you know what you are having yet?" Katie said, seeming interested.

"No, not yet, but soon we will."

"You are going to be a daddy. How awesome is that?"

"I know. Well, let us go. We need to call some more people. I just wanted you to know because you are one of my oldest friends," Aaron said.

"Of course. Again, I'm so happy for you two." That phrase again, "oldest friend." Katie hated the phrase.

Katie hung up the phone. It was cemented in now. They would never be together. They would never share any moments like they had. They would never end up together. Aaron would always be with his wife. Given that Aaron came from a broken home, she knew he wanted stability with his child. Katie finally realized she was going to be Aaron's oldest friend forever.

CHAPTER 13

After Katie learned of Aaron having a child, she did the only thing she knew that would help her stop thinking about Aaron: she worked. Katie would spend every minute she could at work or working extra duty. She believed as long as she was bringing money in and she had her career, everything would balance itself out. Katie was working so much she started to burn herself out. As she felt the burnout, she started to hate the job she once loved.

Law enforcement became routine to Katie. It was the same things over and over again. She had changed different jobs within the department, and when that didn't work, she thought changing to a different agency would work. It never did though; but Katie didn't realize she just needed to slow down and deal with her past, all of it—her family life, her job stressors—and heal from the relationship she had with Aaron over the years. She didn't though; she kept working.

Overly independent would be an understatement to describe how Katie was at times. Katie continued to depend on and trust only herself. She pushed a lot of people who wanted to know her away, females and males. She began to take on the persona of a hardened "bitch" to the world, because it felt like it protected her from everyone who could possibly come in and destroy her. Sarcastic was her middle name, but she always used sarcasm in a way to make people laugh.

Months would keep rolling by. Katie had finished her bachelor's degree and had started her master's degree. Not that she needed them for the job she was doing, but it was something Katie felt she needed to do. To the outside, she was thought to be smart, but Katie didn't feel it. She was so lost; she was truly trying to find her purpose and protecting herself in the process. It was her way of shoving every bit of emotion down and locking it away. In her eyes, it was her protection. And every now and then, she would receive an email from Aaron. It was the unspoken rule—no phone calls, no text messages, only emails.

> Katie,
> I am just checking on you. For some reason I just had this feeling come over me that I needed to each out and see how you are doing. How are you doing? I am gone overseas right now. It seems my whole life that is all I have been doing.
> I just wanted you to know I was thinking about you.
>
> Aaron
>
> Aaron,
> I am doing good. Just working a lot. Keeps me busy and sane. Overseas again, huh? When are you ever home? Be safe over there and always come home.
>
> Always,
> Katie

Katie had changed so much to everyone else, but she remained the Katie that she was with Aaron. Somehow, the emails from Aaron seemed to make Katie feel human and like someone understood her. He made Katie feel not so alone in the world. Aaron was right though; they always knew when things weren't right with each other. It was always so hard to explain, but they just knew. Katie always blew it off as they had known each other too long. They were friends, and Aaron was being a friend the best way he knew how, checking on her and making sure she did not need anything. Neither mentioned Aaron's wife or his child. It was always a very neutral conversation, but the love was always in each other's emails. Nothing special was said, but it was a special bond they shared.

> Katie,
> How are you today, Katie? I have to keep checking on you. I'm worried about you. I was thinking, I am coming home soon. Would you like to get some coffee again? Same place?
>
> Love,
> Aaron
>
> Aaron,
> Why do you worry about me so much? I am fine. Just staying busy, making the time pass. Remember, I am a big girl now, Aaron. I'm not as sheltered as I once was. I'm changing. I don't know if you would even want to be around me anymore. :) But yes, I would like to get coffee with you when you get back. Just let me know and we will make it happen.
>
> Love Always,
> Katie

The emails continued, picking at each other back and forth. Now in their thirties, they had twenty years of history together. They weren't a couple, just friends. Each knew they could tell the other anything, and no matter what was said, each would not think anything less of the other. They were forever bonded through the trials in their life, and they would always have each other even if there was no one else to count on.

Katie sat down on her couch and looked up at the ceiling in complete silence. Her dog was beside her as she thought about what her life had become. She was now in her thirties, was divorced, and was alone. She had friends, but she pushed them away, not wanting to leave the compounds of home. She thought about the selfish, bratty person she was her whole life; she was embarrassed. Katie was tired of feeling the way she did. She thought to herself, *How can I live the rest of my life like this and be able to deal with it? I'm in my thirties. I'm not old.* She decided she had to change. She wanted to be a different person.

Katie got up from the couch and went to her desk, taking a piece of paper. She started to write down her goals and what she wanted to change in her life. Katie was finishing up her graduate degree and would have more time to work just on herself.

Katie started trying new things to see if they would interest her. Katie began analyzing her life, every aspect of it, and how each aspect stopped her from where she wanted to be. She pushed herself to get out with the friends she once had, even at times she did not want to. Katie met new people and started volunteering. She had it set in her mind to be a better person and to inspire others.

Even men started to notice Katie. Katie had a brick fortress around her heart, but she was nice and kindly declined and continued focusing on her career and finishing her graduate degree. As time progressed, Katie did eventually begin to have more male friends in her life. Not the relationship type but friends. She would hang out with them and their girlfriends if they had them at the time, just to get out. She had nothing she needed to go home to, so sometimes she would crash on their couches. She was one of the guys of course, nothing more.

One of her friends, Jason, became her close confidant. Jason went through a bad breakup in the recent months, and he was pretty heartbroken. Katie and Jason would talk about Jason's girlfriend and Aaron. Both came to a lot of realizations, and both understood the other's situations. Katie and Jason would drive and park in the middle of nowhere like Katie and Aaron had done many years ago. Both found comfort in the fact they had loved to the fullest but fell short and one day wanted to feel that again. They kept each other company, cooking together and spending time together. They were helping the other to get over or live with the fact they weren't with the ones they loved. The two ended up getting too close, Katie would come to realize months later. During one of their outings, Jason leaned over and kissed her, in front of everyone to see. It was the start of a turbulent relationship built off a love both didn't have for each other. It lasted a month until one night Jason began to get upset about his ex-girlfriend. Katie looked at Jason and said, "Maybe you should call her and try to work things out." Jason thought it would never work out, but Katie said she thought it would be perfect. Jason, being extremely intoxicated at the time of his confession, was undressed of his clothing and placed in bed. Katie let herself out of the door, and that was the end of their summer fling.

Katie of course still spoke with Jason, but it was never the same. Jason ended up getting back with his ex-girlfriend, and things seemed to be going well. Katie had become the matchmaker, but that was okay too. She was still working on herself. Katie believed she was damaged goods; too much for one person to handle. A great friend who would do anything for anyone but just not the person to be in a relationship with. After her summer fling, Katie would go out with cute guys who asked her out, but the minute they showed interest, Katie would stop all contact with them. She would always brush it off. "I'm too hard to handle" or "I would run all over you."

The summer would be spent with a lot of lessons learned for Katie. That summer, she would realize that she was only going out with individuals she could control, minus Jason. Katie realized that she had a fear of letting anyone close to her who could possibly leave her. She was playing it safe with anyone she felt could possibly hurt her. Katie tried to heal from Aaron; she even realized she would not even date anyone close to Aaron's height. She did recognize that she always looked for Aaron in others and that she needed to find someone totally different. Looking for Aaron in others was only going to lead her into a divorce again or she would leave them when she started to feel anything from them.

Katie continued to excel in her career and dated a few people, and she was free. She was free to have peace when she wanted it, and she had the freedom to go out if she wanted to. Her newfound freedom and the attention she was getting made her feel happy. She was realizing that she would never really heal, but she did know she needed to live. Katie felt that she was doing pretty good. She was starting to help women she knew going through similar situations, and she felt that it was her purpose.

Although Katie was embracing single life and her newfound purpose, which kept her pretty busy, Aaron would pop in her mind at times. Nothing special would be going on, but she would start to think about the memories between the two of them. She couldn't help but analyze each and every time they had together and wonder what went wrong. What could have been if she had made different choices? Katie tried to remind herself that it never worked out because it was never meant to be. It was the only way for her to come back to the reality that Aaron was married with a child and thousands of miles away. But every time she would tell herself this, it seemed the universe pulled them back together. Katie, after telling herself Aaron wasn't coming back and that she needed to move forward with her life and her purpose, would get an email.

> Katie,
> I was sitting here thinking about you, and for some reason, I felt that something was wrong, and I wanted to check in on you. Are you doing okay? I just wanted you to know that I am thinking about you and that you crossed my mind.
>
> Love,
> Aaron
>
> Aaron,
> Hey there. I am doing good. I was actually thinking of you the other day and wondering what you were doing, if

you were home. I hope you are doing good and being safe.

Always,
Katie

Katie,
Yes, I am doing good. I am actually home. What do you think about getting some coffee? We haven't done that in a while.
Aaron

Aaron,
Yes, that would be great, it's been too long. When and where?

Katie

Katie,
How about our norm? I can drive up tomorrow if you are okay with it and not doing anything. 9?

Aaron

Katie knew she had to work tomorrow, but instead of telling Aaron she had to work, she replied.

Aaron,
That will be perfect. I will see you then.

Katie

Katie knew she could get her work covered and just blame not being there on an appointment. The two had met several times at a coffee shop.

It was busy all of the time, and the two kind of annoyed the waitress who would be waiting on them. Katie and Aaron would sit for hours talking, only drinking coffee, never ordering anything more.

Katie had a surge of happiness throughout her whole body. She knew they were only having coffee together, and they were friends, but just knowing they would be in the same room together made Katie happy. It made Katie's whole attitude change from just going through the motions to one of hope and faith. As if the thought of being in the same room as Aaron was going to make everything that she was going through go away. Katie knew that she still had a long way to go, but in the moments leading up to seeing him again, she found peace with her life.

The next day, Katie walked into the coffee shop to see Aaron already sitting down. She smiled and slid into the booth, sitting directly across from Aaron. "Hey, you," Katie said, smiling.

Aaron smiled. "Hey, you."

Katie could tell something was on Aaron's mind, and something was bothering him. "So what have you been up to?" Katie said.

"Not much. I just got back from overseas a little while ago. For the most part good," Aaron said, barely making eye contact with Katie.

"Okay, you're full of crap," Katie said, laughing. "What's wrong? Is Sam okay?" Katie asked more seriously.

"Yeah, Sam is fine. My wife is divorcing me," Aaron said.

"Oh, Aaron, I am so sorry. What is going to happen with Sam? What are you going to do?" Katie was devastated for Aaron. He seemed to be truly happy each time she spoke to him by email. Katie did not understand what happened. She thought they both were happy. Looking at Aaron, Katie knew he was completely crushed.

"I don't know yet. We are still working out the details. I think I am going to have Sam," Aaron said.

"I'm so sorry, Aaron. I don't know what to say. Can I do anything for you? I don't know what to say. I'm shocked," Katie said. Her heart was truly breaking for Aaron. She could feel how heartbroken Aaron was. She could feel all of the broken dreams and hopes for a forever with one person. She wanted to take his pain away, she wanted to fix it, but she knew she couldn't.

Aaron looked at Katie. "No, but being here with you helps."

Katie smiled and sarcastically said, "Well, I'm glad I can do that for you."

Aaron let out a laugh; and Katie felt hope, hope that somehow, she could help Aaron come out of his dark place. Somehow help him to see that he can get past divorce and the abandonment he felt.

Aaron changed the subject, and the two talked for another two hours. They caught up on life and talked about their deepest secrets, being divorcees, and the future of who they wanted to be. Katie and Aaron could talk about anything, and they were most of all always friends, friends who could trust each other with their darkest secrets.

"I'm scared of being alone forever," Katie said.

"You're kidding me, right? Like how many guys have you already married in your thirties?" Aaron said, joking with Katie.

"Haha, Aaron. I'm like a celebrity. I have to keep rotating them out. Seriously, I don't want to be alone forever, Aaron. I'm going to be the old cat lady. I'm too hard to handle," Katie said, being serious.

Aaron smiled, knowing Katie would never be alone. "Katie, you will find your next victim. I guarantee you will find someone. You are not as hard to handle as you put out there."

"Aren't you worried about being alone?" Katie asked Aaron.

"Well, I don't mind being alone, Katie. You know that I've always been like that. I don't think I will always be alone, but if I am, I am okay with that too," Aaron said.

"Am I crazy for thinking like I do?"

"Katie, you just think too much about it. Let things just happen and stop always searching for that next person. You are trying to make things fit."

"Oh, look who has the relationship advice," Katie said, smiling.

"Well, I think I am good at some things," Aaron said, smiling.

Katie looked down at her watch. "Dang it, Aaron, I didn't realize we were here so long. I got to get going. I am sorry."

"Yeah, I have to get back too," Aaron said, upset Katie already had to leave.

They both got up and walked outside. "It was good to see you, Katie. Thank you for meeting me. This is exactly what I needed."

"Yes, it was really good to see you too, Aaron. You had a great idea to get coffee at this place," Katie said, smiling.

"I got to get a hug before you go," Aaron said.

Katie smiled and raised her arms, and Aaron picked her up to hug her. After what felt like an eternity, Aaron put Katie back down.

"We need to do this more often," Katie said.

"Yeah, we do," Aaron said.

"See you soon then?" Katie said, walking to her car.

"Yeah, see you soon," Aaron said as he watched Katie make it to her car and get inside it before walking to his own vehicle and getting into it.

———————— • ——— • ————————

"So you saw Aaron?" Katie's mom asked during one of their Sunday dinners.

"Yes." Katie had let it slip out to her mom that she was going to see Aaron during one of their recent conversations. Katie and her mom had mended the turbulent relationship that they once had. Not living in the house was a help.

"So what is going on with you two?"

"Nothing. We are just really good friends. I guess we have known each other for so long, it is just easy to talk to each other. I mean, it's been twenty years."

Katie's mom could see it written all over Katie's face. Katie was still in love with Aaron after all these years. "Do you still love him?"

"Hmmm, yeah, I guess." Katie knew she did but wasn't willing to tell her mother the whole truth.

"You know your dad and I were friends for years before we started dating."

"Yeah, you told me that before. Weird."

"You know, I was crazy about a boy, kind of like you were with Aaron before. It was a long time ago."

Katie was confused. "What?" This was the first time her mom ever mentioned anyone she dated besides her dad.

"His name was Michael. I was crazy about him, and he was crazy about me."

"What happened then if you both were crazy about each other?" Katie was curious.

"I was younger than him. He graduated and went off to college. On the weekends, he would come down and see me. He also worked. We had a dance at school one weekend, and Michael made it down to go to the dance, but when he got to my house, he said he was tired and didn't want to go. I got mad, and we started arguing. I left and went to the dance, and when I got back, he had left. It was the last time I talked to him or saw him. I was stubborn back then too, and I didn't realize at that young of an age adulthood and responsibilities."

"Did you ever try to look for him?"

"I did after the internet started, but I never found him. I heard he was married and had kids."

Katie didn't know what to say. "Wow, kind of in shock and wondering why you are telling me this."

Katie's mom was quiet for a moment and then said, "Be a dreamer, Katie. If you know, hang on to hope and have faith. And stop being so damn stubborn like your mom."

Katie smiled. "I am trying, but I have it naturally from one of my parents."

Katie and her mom continued to talk, never mentioning the conversation again. In fact, it was never mentioned after that time. It started to make sense to Katie. Her mom was trying to protect her from Aaron who was going through a transition, from being a kid to adulthood. She was trying to let Katie be a kid for just a few more years.

CHAPTER 14

Life happened, and Katie and Aaron fell back into their normal lives. They continued to talk and email each other, but it was months since the last time they saw each other. There was no talk of a relationship, only a friendship that they had started twenty years earlier as kids. They would laugh so hard they would cry, and of course they would have the deep conversations of their hopes and dreams for the future. Although the two were living only an hour away from each other, they never spoke about meeting up for coffee since the last time they saw each other.

"So, Katie, you are coming tonight, right?" Katie's friend Maria said.

"Maria, I don't really know Ryan like that. I would be intruding," Katie said, really not wanting to go out.

"He's a damn cop. You have worked with him. I'm coming to pick you up at six," Maria said.

"Yes, he is a cop. I have worked with him, but this is weird. You just don't want to go, and you are forcing me to go."

"I'll be there at six," Maria said, hanging up the phone.

Maria was there a little after six. As Katie got in Maria's car, Maria was on the phone. "Well, just come on anyway." Maria had a way of always talking people into things. Everyone loved Maria, and she was definitely fun to be around.

"Who was that victim?" Katie said with a grin.

"That was Taylor. He's a cop. I don't think you know him. He's a nice guy. He just . . . I don't know how to describe him. Like you can't get off the phone with him," Maria said.

"So he won't shut the fuck up?" Katie said.

Maria burst into hysterical laughter. "Not what I was thinking, but he does like to talk."

The dinner was just as Katie thought. She felt weird even though everyone at the table knew of her. Katie had gained a reputation as a great cop, and people respected her. Katie herself didn't feel that way; she was just doing her job and trying to do the right thing.

As usual, Maria was the life of the party. Katie laughed as Maria became alive mingling with everyone. At one time she was sitting next to Katie but had since bounced around the table. Strategically, Taylor was sitting right next to Katie, and Katie was making small talk with Taylor. He seemed nice, and they could hold a conversation together. After dinner, everyone had scattered throughout the restaurant. The restaurant also had a dance area for when they played music, and several tables surrounded it. Katie and Maria found a table, and Taylor managed to follow them down to the table. As Maria started to see people she knew, she was off again to leave Katie and Taylor sitting alone. Taylor started to get Katie into a conversation, but of course, Katie did not like shallow conversations. She always found them pretty lame.

"So how long have you been a cop?" Taylor asked.

"Ten years," Katie said.

"What kind of cases do you like to work on?"

"All kinds, drug and homicide cases, I guess."

"Do you live by yourself?"

"Yes."

This went on for about ten minutes. Questions that Katie felt did not matter one way or another. Katie felt those questions were just questions that were answered during the course of time, not the most important things to know at first. She was getting bored and fast, but she couldn't leave because Maria had driven her, and she was off still having fun.

"So have you been married?"

"Yes," Katie said.

"Is your family from here?"

"My parents live here, but we are originally from Florida."

"Are you going to move back to Florida?"

"I've thought about it, but my parents are here, and I don't want to leave them alone because they are getting older."

"Do you have any siblings?"

"Yes, there are four of us."

Katie answered all the questions but was turned partially away from Taylor watching Maria. As Taylor was asking his questions, a man came down and sat beside Katie. Taylor and Katie both looked at him in shock. The man, halfway drunk, started talking to Katie. Taylor leaned over to Katie. "Do you know him?"

"No, I don't know who that is."

As the man continued to talk, Katie was trying to be nice but about had enough. Katie turned to Taylor, and Taylor said, "Come here." Taylor leaned in and kissed Katie on the lips.

Surprisingly, Katie kissed him back. The man got up and walked away, and Taylor and Katie laughed.

Maria came back to the table. "You ready?"

Katie jumped up. "Yep."

Maria turned to Taylor. "I am taking some people home. Do you need a ride since you have been drinking?"

Taylor said, "Yeah, I'll pick up my car tomorrow."

"Okay," Maria said as she bopped off.

Katie and Taylor sat in the back of Maria's car. They talked about meaningless things, but Taylor was actually pretty fun. He also had pretty eyes, green but pretty. Katie and Taylor were the last people that Maria took home. As they pulled up to Katie's house, Katie got out of the vehicle. Taylor got out of the vehicle and met Katie halfway around the car.

"Can I get your phone number?" Taylor asked.

"Yeah, sure," Katie said, giving Taylor her number before she said, "See you around," and walked inside.

As Katie walked upstairs and started to get ready for bed, she received a text message from Taylor. "It was really nice to meet you tonight."

Katie replied, "Yeah."

Taylor began to pursue Katie heavily. He wanted to do a lot of things with Katie and all of the time. They got along well, but Katie felt she didn't want to get married again. She was having fun though; that was all that mattered. Katie liked how she did not have to wonder if Taylor liked her. He was always texting her, he was always calling her, and he always wanted to do things with her. Katie did not have to question what she and Taylor were; he wanted her and only her.

Of course, as soon as Katie could possibly be considered as dating someone, she got an email from Aaron.

>Katie,
>I haven't heard from you in a while, and I just wanted to check on you. How are you doing? I was thinking it was about time to grab coffee. What do you think?
>
>Love,
>Aaron

>Aaron,
>Well of course. It has been too long as usual. Tell me the time and place and I'll be there. What have you been up to

anyway? You disappeared. Did you go overseas again?

Always,
Katie

Katie,
It is a long story. We will catch up. I will be bringing John with me. How about tomorrow at 9?

Aaron

Aaron,
Yeah, that is good with me. Who's John?

Katie

Katie,
He's my other son. I had another child.

Aaron

Katie read the email again. *Aaron had another child? Wow, that is crazy, not what I was expecting. It should be interesting to talk about how that happened.*

The next day, Katie met Aaron at their normal coffee spot. As usual, Aaron was already inside sitting down with John. Katie's heart melted when she saw John. He was the most precious little baby. Katie was a little nervous with how tiny John was. She had not been around a baby in a long time, but she did great. Maybe it was Aaron being right there with her, knowing that Aaron made her feel safe in any situation.

Katie finally said with a smile, "Well, what have you been up to, besides having another baby!"

Aaron laughed. "Not much. The boys take up a lot of time."

"I can imagine that. So how did this happen? Obviously I have missed some things," Katie said with a smile.

"We tried to work things out, and she ended up pregnant. After John was born, she left again."

"So are you two divorced or separated?" Katie asked.

"No, we are divorced," Aaron said adamantly. "What have you been doing, Katie?"

Katie had done a lot of soul-searching the past year. She was working on herself; she was changing her views and how to live her life. She didn't know if she wanted Aaron to know about the darkness she had lived. She didn't want Aaron to know it broke her and she barely survived it.

Before Katie could stop herself, she said, "Aaron, I'm a different person. I've changed. I didn't like who I was or the way I was living. I did a lot of things I shouldn't have and a lot of things I'm not proud of."

"You seem to be the same person you have always been, Katie," Aaron said, reassuring her.

"I'm sorry, Aaron. Sorry for everything I have put you through and everything that I said that was wrong. I was young and just didn't see what I needed to see."

"Katie, we all do things we wish we had not done. I could kick myself for doing some of the stuff I have done."

"I just wish I could go back and have a reset. To start all over again and do things differently," Katie said, looking down.

"You're always going to be my Katie, the same girl I met twenty years ago."

Katie thought about it. It had actually been twenty years since she had met Aaron. It seemed like she just met him but yet had known him forever. The chemistry between them was still there. Katie could feel it, and they weren't doing anything but talking. To Katie, it seemed each time they saw each other, it got stronger and stronger.

"It's hard to believe it has been that long. We were so young when we met," Katie blurted out before she even thought about what she was saying.

"I still love you, Katie. I always have and always will," Aaron said.

Katie looked at Aaron who had been staring at her. "I love you too, Aaron. True soulmates."

Aaron smiled and grabbed Katie's hand from across the table. Katie squeezed Aaron's hand.

"I miss us," Katie confessed. Aaron continued to look at Katie but did not say anything. The two sat in silence until John started to fuss in his seat. Aaron took a bottle out of the bag he brought with him and gave it to John.

"What's your plan now, Katie? You are divorced and not tied down in any way," Aaron said, chuckling.

"You got jokes I see," Katie said with a smile. "You know, I don't really know. I guess keep doing what I am doing. I am back in school again, and we will see where that leads me. What about you?"

"I don't know yet. With two sons, it is hard to do what I was doing, but I will make it work. I always have been good at that. Just don't have it all figured out yet."

"Are you going to stay in Florida?" Katie asked, wanting to know and trying to be incognito. She had already started thinking about future meetings with Aaron in her head.

"Yes, I plan on staying in Florida, Katie. My family is there, and until I have everything figured out, I will need them." Aaron knew where Katie was going with her questioning, but he didn't say anything. His questioning was being incognito about the future and Katie being in it.

Katie and Aaron continued to talk. They talked about Sam, Aaron's older son, and how Aaron and Katie's past had crazy times and fun times. As always, there was never a dull moment between the two, and they always picked up where they left off, as if they had just seen each other last week. Before they knew it, three hours had passed without either of them knowing. John surprisingly had been calm the whole time they were talking. It was like John was rooting for them and letting them have their time, as silly as it seems.

"I better go, Katie. John is going to need a nap and another bottle soon, and I have to drive back," Aaron finally said.

"I understand," Katie said, making funny faces at John. Aaron watched as Katie interacted with John. His heart was full, and he could barely hold back the joy he had inside him at that moment.

"Can you watch him for a minute so I can go start the car to warm it up?"

Katie, still smiling at John, said, "Yes, Dad, I think we got this. We will be fine."

Aaron smiled at Katie as he walked outside to start the car. As he walked out to the car, he could not stop thinking about Katie; she was his person. He always wanted to tell Katie, but he could never think of the perfect words to say. He always froze, as if Katie made him nervous. Aaron wanted to tell Katie he wanted a future with her in it; he wanted kids with her and wanted their life to start together. Aaron knew Katie would feel the same way. He did not doubt it; but for some reason, he felt if he said something, it would change things between him and Katie. As Aaron started walking back into the coffee shop, he saw Katie and John through the window. Katie was still talking to John, playing with him.

When Aaron reached the table, he said, "Were you two plotting against me?"

Katie smiled. "No, we were telling secrets to each other."

"Oh really?" Aaron said, amused.

"Yep, he told me all the dirt on you."

"Of course he did, traitor," Aaron said, looking toward John.

Aaron went to pay the bill, and Katie said, "I got it."

Aaron looked at Katie. "I think I can handle the coffee, Katie. I got it."

Katie was never much for men paying her bill. It always felt weird to her. "Thank you."

Katie, Aaron, and John walked outside. As soon as the cold hit her, Katie began to shake. They walked to Aaron's car to put John in, out of the cold. "Go ahead and get in on the passenger seat," Aaron told Katie, knowing she hated the cold.

Katie climbed into the passenger seat and put her hands by the heater vent to warm them up. She turned around and watched Aaron put John into the car seat before getting in the driver's seat. When he sat down, he turned and looked at Katie.

"It was good to see you. We should do this more," Aaron said.

"Yeah, it's not like we live thousands of miles away anymore," Katie said.

Aaron laughed, knowing it was a reference to when he lived in North Dakota. "No, not that far away anymore."

John began to cry, and Aaron reached behind him to comfort John. When that didn't work, Aaron took John out of the car seat and started to hold him. It did not take long before John was calm in Aaron's arms.

"Can I hold him one more time before you go?" Katie asked.

Aaron handed John to Katie. Katie placed John on her lap and looked at him, talking to him. Aaron watched and smiled as Katie interacted with John, talking to him and kissing his little hands. After a few minutes, Katie handed John back to Aaron who put him back into the car seat.

"Can I get a hug bye?" Aaron asked Katie.

Katie smiled. "Of course."

Aaron hugged Katie tightly. Katie placed her hands on the back of Aaron's head and whispered, "It was so good to see you." Aaron pulled back slightly and placed his hand on Katie's face, pulling her toward him. Aaron kissed Katie's lips. Katie's heart began racing, and she could feel every part of her body tingling. Aaron and Katie pulled back, placing their foreheads together with their eyes closed.

"I'll talk to you soon," Aaron said.

"Yeah," Katie said.

Katie got out of Aaron's car and walked toward her car, getting inside. Aaron waited for Katie to pull out before he followed her out of the parking lot, going the opposite direction. After being out of sight from Aaron, Katie began to smile. They had the same connection that they had twenty years ago, and it felt perfect.

Katie's phone rang, and she looked down. *Shit, it is Taylor.* She answered, "Hello?"

"Hey, what are you up to? I went by your work, and they said you weren't there," he said.

"Yeah, I met with a high school friend I hadn't seen in a long time for coffee," Katie said.

"Oh okay, how did that go?"

"It went good. It was good catching up with them," Katie said without stating if the friend was male or female.

"All right, I was going to come over tonight and hang out," Taylor said.

"I don't know if I'm up for it tonight," Katie said.

"Well, we got to talk about our trip anyway. I won't stay long."

"Okay," Katie said reluctantly.

When Katie got home, she threw her keys down and fell to the couch. Could she and Aaron possibly have a chance? A chance after so many years apart? Would it be the same or even better? Aaron had two boys as well. Katie, although nervous, knew that her coming into the situation would be hard at first; but they could be a family. She adored John, and she knew she would love Sam too. So many thoughts were running through her head, and then she thought of Taylor. What was she going to tell Taylor? He was nice to her and made her laugh, but her heart was always with Aaron, and Katie knew that. She and Taylor hadn't made things official, but they had both spent the night over each other's houses, and they had planned a trip together. Katie knew what she had to do but did not want to hurt anyone.

"So next week, you are going to drive up on Wednesday and spend until Friday and we will head back?" Katie had already cut the trip short and told Taylor she had to work.

"Yeah, I will be there after work on Wednesday," Katie said. Katie had started to distance herself from Taylor. She had already been telling Taylor that things were moving a little faster than she would like. She had already told Taylor she did not know if she wanted a serious relationship or not. Taylor would always change the subject and acted as if her opinion did not matter. It was one of the things Katie was starting to dislike about Taylor.

Katie would get relief from Taylor when she would hear from Aaron. She wanted to tell Aaron about everything, but she did not want him to stop talking to her. She did not want Aaron to leave because he thought she wanted Taylor. Katie felt like she was living a double life and wanted a fresh start. She wanted a life with Aaron; she knew that. She had next week, and then she would tell Taylor she could not be with him, that her heart was not in it. She knew it would hurt Taylor, but she had a sneaky suspicion it would not take Taylor very long to move on, as Taylor seemed to like women and his job way too much.

Wednesday came, and Katie took the drive to the beach. Not her favorite beach but one Taylor had picked.

"Katie, so glad you could make it," Taylor said as she got out of her car. She felt like a guest in his world.

"Hey, Taylor," Katie said.

"Let's get your stuff inside, and then I have plans to go fishing with some friends, and then we will go out to eat around 5:00 PM. So be ready at that time."

"Okay," Katie said, thinking, *What the hell am I supposed to do while you are gone?*

Katie got her things inside of the hotel room, and Taylor kissed her bye. "See you soon," he said and walked out of the door. Katie sat down on the bed. She thought about Aaron and wondered what he was doing at the time. She wondered if Aaron was thinking about her and if he was really wanting things to be different this time or whether it was just another thought like they made before but never happened. Katie did have doubts, as it had been so many years of things between her and Aaron not working. *Can we actually make it work?* Katie thought. Katie just knew if the two of them could be on the same page, it would work. The chemistry, the connection. It was like Katie could feel Aaron around her, even when they weren't together. She just couldn't let Aaron go again; she had to try just one more time.

At 5:00 PM, as Taylor said, he came back to the room to pick Katie up. They ate at a fancy restaurant that Katie thought was overpriced. She would have been happier sitting by the water at a restaurant in a laid-back atmosphere. Taylor talked as he always did, and Katie sat and listened. When Katie could, she would break into the conversation. Taylor did make her laugh, and he did make her smile. Katie couldn't help but think this was going to be one of the last dinners, if not the last dinner, they would have together.

Katie was hoping to take a walk on the beach once they finished dinner, but Taylor wanted to go back to the room. So they did, and Taylor laid down on the bed and turned on the television. Katie laid down next to Taylor and tried to be interested in the television show he was watching. Taylor was watching another military movie, movies that Katie never thought were "entertainment" because of Aaron. He never asked her opinion on what she wanted to watch; that was just Taylor. Taylor never wanted to have long, deep conversations either. He always would turn on the television to pass time together. Katie kept thinking, *Not much longer.*

The week after Taylor and Katie got back, Katie distanced herself from Taylor. She began telling him she was not ready for a relationship, and she would pick fights when she could, hoping that Taylor would get tired of it and leave. He didn't though, and Katie was exhausted from the stress. She had been exhausted a lot lately, and she thought it was from Taylor and then also speaking with Aaron. Katie had so much going on, she didn't even realize she had missed her period until she started thinking more about her being tired and queasy. Katie thought, *Oh my god, no. This isn't happening. It can't be.* Katie tried to remember the last time she had her period, and she just couldn't. She went to her bathroom and looked in the cabinet. There was a pregnancy test, out of date, but a test.

Katie took the test and walked out of the room and sat on the bed. She couldn't be pregnant; she hadn't even told Taylor she loved him. She was worrying for no reason; she was never really on a schedule, and her cycle had always been off and late. Taylor didn't even want kids; he told that to Katie when they started dating.

Katie walked back into the bathroom; her heart was racing. She looked down after taking a deep breath, and the tears started to fill her eyes. She walked out of the bathroom and sat down on the bed, bringing her knees to her chest. She wrapped her arms around her legs and buried her head in her arms and cried. She was pregnant.

CHAPTER 15

After finding out she was pregnant, Katie stopped talking to Aaron. She stopped returning his phone calls, stopped answering his text messages, and stopped replying to his emails. She couldn't tell Aaron; she was embarrassed. She hadn't even told Taylor yet. Katie knew she had to tell Taylor. She had decided she was going to keep the baby. She could not kill a baby just because it was unplanned. In her mind, she was scared but okay with the idea of having a child. Katie felt it was a sign that maybe she was supposed to be with Taylor. She felt it was a sign that she needed a child to love.

"What's been up with you tonight?" Taylor asked Katie as he watched TV.

"Nothing really," Katie said.

"You seem like something is up with you."

"I got to tell you something."

Taylor turned to Katie. "Okay."

"I missed my period, and I may be pregnant," Katie blurted out.

Taylor looked at Katie surprised, and regret was written all over his face. "Did you take a test?"

"No, but I bought some, and they are in the bathroom." Katie couldn't tell him that she had already taken three tests, all of which were positive.

Taylor jumped up from the bed. "Well, take the test!" he said, irritated.

"What if I am pregnant?" Katie asked, reading Taylor.

"Well, I don't want kids. We will get it handled," Taylor said.

"Like abortion?" Katie said, shocked, as she got up to go and take the test.

"We can't have a kid. We aren't prepared for that," Taylor said.

Katie took the test and came back and sat on the bed. Taylor was pacing back and forth. "Maybe we should have the baby."

"No, we can't financially, and we don't need a baby," Taylor said. Katie could see on his face how nervous he was. Taylor walked into the bathroom; Katie already knew what he was going to see. He came back out and sat down on the bed. "You're pregnant."

Katie managed to say, "Okay."

Taylor sat on the bed. He turned to the television and started watching TV. "I'll get it handled in the morning. I'll figure it out." Katie laid down on the bed, turning away from Taylor. She didn't want to have an abortion. She was not going to do that, but she was not going to argue with Taylor about it. Katie closed her eyes and fell asleep.

The next day, Taylor left for work before Katie got up. Katie got up and began getting ready for work. Her phone started ringing, and it was Taylor. "Hello," Katie said.

"I found a clinic in Florida you can go to. All you have to do is call and make an appointment. I will pay for it."

Katie was angered by the remarks. "I am not getting an abortion. You don't have to stay. You can go, but I am not going to do that."

"We talked about this last night and decided," Taylor said, taken aback by Katie's anger.

"No, Taylor, you decided, not me. I am not doing it, so if you have to go, go." Katie hung up the phone. She was furious that Taylor's decision to deal with the pregnancy was to terminate it. She did not need him; she did not need anyone. Thirty minutes later, Taylor called back.

"Hello," Katie said, irritated.

"If we are going to do this, we are all in," Taylor said.

Katie said, "Okay, but you don't have to stay. I will be fine."

Taylor remained silent until he finally hung up.

The next seven months seemed to be hectic as both Taylor and Katie had not expected to be parents. As much as Katie and Taylor weren't expecting a pregnancy, their families weren't either. After the adjustment, the families were happy to be adding a baby into the family—a little girl that everyone agreed to name Emma.

Katie was trying to get used to the sequence of events that was happening in her life. She was excited about Emma but felt her life was a shit show. Taylor and she had what they call a shotgun wedding at the courthouse. Taylor and Katie were more friends than anything else. Since Katie told Taylor she was not aborting the baby, Taylor had been more distant than before. Although he stayed true to his promise of being all in, he was only all in with living together and getting married. But Katie felt it was a sign that she needed to go through this with Taylor and that there was a reason that everything happened the way it did. Katie hoped to one day know what the reason was and how everything would be put together in her life. As for now, she was just confused.

Katie had not spoken to Aaron since finding out she was pregnant; he did not even know. He probably thought Katie just didn't want to be with him anymore. She just couldn't tell him; she still was not ready. Katie did not know if she could ever tell Aaron until after they baby was born or maybe even years after that. She just could not think of the perfect words to say. Aaron had stopped calling and texting about a month into Katie ignoring him. Katie knew that Aaron had given up on them rekindling anything they could have had. Plus, Katie was just embarrassed to even tell Aaron. She felt horrible for what happened, and she wished she had at least told Aaron she was seeing other people, but she had led Aaron to believe by her actions that it was only him. Katie wondered if Aaron even cared about what happened, if he even thought about why. Then Katie checked her email, and she had her answer.

> Katie,
> I have been thinking about you and
> wondering how you are. I tried to call

and text, but I've never heard from you.
Was it something I said, or I did? I just
need to know, no matter what it is. I hope
to hear from you soon.

Love,
Aaron

Katie knew she had to tell him. So she hit reply.

Aaron,
There is so much going on. Aaron, I'm
pregnant and having a little girl. After
I saw you last time, I found out I was
pregnant soon after. I just couldn't
tell you; I couldn't bring you into this
situation. The dad and I are going to
try and make it work for the baby. I just
didn't know what else to do. I'm so sorry,
Aaron. I just have to do what I think is
right. I love you always.

Katie

Katie hit send and knew that was probably the last interaction she
would have with Aaron. She knew that would hurt him. She knew there
would never be a way to make it up to Aaron. To Katie's surprise, Aaron
responded a few days later.

Katie,
You should have talked to me. We would
have dealt with it. I would have raised her
like she was my own. I understand the
choices you made, but I wish you would

have told me. I will and do respect your decisions.

I love you, Katie,
Aaron

Katie closed her email with tears in her eyes. She felt she had to get her life together. She had to raise Emma like a princess, and she had to choose to be happy. It was not how she expected it to happen, but it did, and there was a reason. She had to try, and she had to do it for Emma.

The next few years flew by for Katie. She was busy raising Emma. Katie did everything for Emma as Taylor kept his promise to be in it together but not when it came to doing anything but staying married to Katie. The more Katie pushed Taylor to try to make it work, the more Taylor pushed her away, until Katie finally gave up. They were roommates raising the child they had together, and Katie began to believe this was her karma for all of the relationships she had in her life. She felt this was what she deserved, and she was okay with it as long as she had Emma. That was Katie's joy.

"We live like roommates."

"Well, if you would communicate with me, it would work."

"Communicate, I've tried, Taylor. It's like you don't care. Are you okay with the way this marriage is?"

"I'm not an affectionate person. I just provide. That is how I show love."

Katie was so frustrated but bit her tongue. Taylor never took care of Emma or had to because he wasn't consistent, and Katie didn't trust him with the responsibility of Emma. Taylor provided nothing but rent to her. They even lived in separate rooms. It was something Katie never experienced in a relationship, but she felt she needed to stay in it for Emma. She didn't want Emma to grow up in a broken home.

Katie thought of Aaron sometimes still. She thought about the times they had together and the last day she saw Aaron. She wondered what

Aaron was doing and what was happening in his own life raising the two boys alone. She wondered if Aaron had forgotten about her or if he still thought about her at times. It drove her crazy at times until Katie couldn't take it anymore.

> Aaron,
> I was thinking about you today and about the past. Why do things always have to be complicated? I want to know why. Why did it have to be like this? I have loved you since I was a teenager. Why couldn't we be together? I'm sorry, I'm having a weak moment. I love you and am thinking about you.
>
> Always,
> Katie

Katie hit send. She got her thoughts out of her mind for now, and she would be okay. Katie did not think she would hear from Aaron, but at least he knew she was thinking about him. To Katie's surprise, a few months later, she heard from Aaron.

> Katie,
> It was good to hear from you. Katie, I wondered that for a long time, but I stopped asking myself that a long time ago. I just hold on tight to the memories that we do have together. I cherish all of them.
> Katie, I love you and I will as long as I breathe. Can we see each other when we can? Let's take the little bit of time we have and spend it together when I am home.

I love you,
Aaron

Katie read Aaron's email again. She was shocked at his response, not expecting it. Katie closed her computer, not knowing how to respond. Yes, she had asked questions to Aaron about why, but she was not expecting his response. She was expecting a cold response or not a response at all. A few weeks later, she had another email from Aaron.

Katie,
Today has been a rough day for me. I watch the people over here do the most horrific things you can imagine, and I couldn't do anything. I don't think people understand the evil in these people.
I need you, Katie.
Can I see you when I come home? I will be home soon.

Love Always,
Aaron

Katie closed the computer. She couldn't meet with Aaron; she knew that. Katie knew the spark would happen. She knew she would put herself in a situation she did not need to be in, especially with Emma. It wasn't just her anymore. But Katie knew that Aaron needed her. She could feel it. She knew whatever he was experiencing overseas, it was bad.

Aaron,
I know it was. I watch old news videos about 9/11 yesterday. Now that I am older, it has more meaning. Of course, it reminds me of you fighting a war that no one wants to talk about.

I know I have not seen the evil you have, but I see a lot of evil. I just don't understand how people can be so evil. The world is changing, and I don't think I am ready for it to.

I know you have found a way to deal with things you see a long time ago, but I am here if you ever need me. Know that.

I love you. Come home safe.

Love,
Katie

Katie hit send on the email. She closed the computer and couldn't help but think of how hard it was for Aaron. He was away from his boys and away from everything normal in his life. He was fighting for a country that didn't even want to admit how many military men and women were over fighting for them to be free. Fighting for what they thought was right. Fighting for all those people who died on 9/11.

After sending that email, Katie did not hear from Aaron. She continued living her life as she had. She and Taylor remained roommates, and she did everything she could for Emma. Katie kept herself busy to stay faithful and to make Emma proud of her.

Katie started to excel at her job, surpassing any expectation she ever had of moving up. She supervised a group of people now and felt a passion for helping others who enjoyed law enforcement as she once had. Katie was pulling away from the love she once had for it. She was almost twenty years into it, but the older she got, the more she realized it pulled her away from the most important aspect of her life, Emma. She didn't know how to get out of a career she had done for so many years. Everyone she knew was in law enforcement. It was like one huge family, a bond that people on the outside did not understand. She continued to do her job as no one knew her feelings, and she was good at it. It all came crashing down on her when one of her youngest agents passed away. Katie was crushed and felt she was to blame as she knew the horrors of COVID-19 but still sent her agents out. It felt like a gamble to Katie, and she was gambling with every single one of her agents' lives.

The death of one of the youngest agents led Katie to meet his parents. Katie felt drawn to his parents. She even left Emma for a week to go honor him with his parents in Washington, DC, at the police memorial. The week was humbling for Katie, and she realized she was part of a group of individuals who were family. It was a tough career, but how could she leave the brother/sisterhood?

While sitting in her hotel room between events in Washington, Katie felt the urge to start writing. To start writing her story into a book, a book telling her story to help others who were going through the same thing she had. Katie opened her computer.

I'm no one special. I'm just a mom living an ordinary life in a small town . . .

Before Katie knew it, she had written the introduction and chapter one and was halfway through the second chapter. Katie left Washington with a renewed spirit and a purpose that she didn't have when she arrived. Katie was ready to grow and to be more than she ever thought she would be.

After returning from Washington, she continued to write, not telling anyone she was writing a book. She would stay on the computer for hours at a time writing. Taylor never asked any questions as he was either off doing something by himself or watching television, not paying attention to Katie. Between writing her book and taking care of Emma, Katie would have to go out of town to work riots that were breaking out due to COVID-19 and the pandemic at hand. Katie stayed focused on the job while she was gone but hated to leave Emma behind each and every time. The way to cope for Katie was not to think about home; it made the weeks easier. Katie pondered whether Aaron handled it the same way each time he had to leave his boys. She believed they both probably thought the same way about it.

It had been a while since she had heard from Aaron, but Aaron would send emails every so often to Katie. When he did, it was a short email.

Katie,
I wanted to check on you. Protect yourself
and your family.

Aaron

Katie would respond to each one.

Aaron,
We are doing good. Are you working
or off?

Katie

Katie,
I was thinking about you today. I don't
know if you got my last email. I just have
a feeling something is wrong and wanted
to check on you.
Boys are doing good; they are growing.
I don't know if I will ever hear from you
again.

Love,
Aaron

Katie could tell something was wrong with Aaron. His emails were
never like that, and Katie worried what was going on with Aaron.

Aaron,
I am sorry. Things have just been busy.
I know that is not an excuse as we make
time for what we want, but please forgive
me. With work and Emma going to
school, I am worn out by the end of the

day. Emma and I are doing good. It's
crazy how big she is getting and how time
has flown by. It doesn't seem real. Before
I know it, she will be gone. We always
know when something is wrong with the
other. True soulmates.

I love you, Aaron. Please stay safe.

Always,
Katie

Katie sent the email and sat back thinking of Aaron. Where was time
going? Katie always though that they would be going through life together,
getting old together, having kids together; but here they were, years later,
still sending emails and trying to catch up on life whenever they could.
It just seemed not right; it seemed unfair, but Katie had to come to terms
with the fact that her life was exactly how it was supposed to be. She was
lucky to have Emma, lucky to be writing a book, and lucky to have grown
so much. Katie was in a good place for the most part. She was happy but
felt she was still missing something in her life. Katie was determined to
figure it out though, and she would.

As Katie sat on the couch one night with Taylor beside her, she hit send
on her book. She had sent her book to an editor whom she had chosen to
edit it and make corrections. She looked over at Taylor who was sitting on
the couch watching TV.

"I wrote a book," Katie said.

Taylor looked over at her. "What, a children's book?"

"No, a book about my journey and how to get through it for other
women."

Taylor was shocked. "When did you write that?" he asked.

"I started it when I went to Washington, and I just finished it and sent
it to the editor," Katie said.

"Like you are going to publish it?" Taylor asked, still in shock.

"Yeah, I want to help other women. I want to help them get through it. I started a group to help women and have been helping them for about a year now."

"Why haven't you said anything? This is the first time I am hearing of it," Taylor said, questioning Katie.

"Well, I didn't know if I was going to publish the book, and I figured it wasn't that big of a deal. I hope if I can sell one a week, it will help just that one other person," Katie said proudly.

Taylor appeared concerned. "I mean, writing a book is not easy. Do you think anyone will buy it?"

Katie opened the draft of her book. "Here, read the introduction." Katie got up to start cooking. Taylor sat on the couch reading the words off Katie's computer. Katie cooked dinner and walked back to where Taylor was sitting on the couch and said, "Dinner is ready."

Taylor got up, bringing the computer into the kitchen. He set it down on the counter in the kitchen. "Obviously, I didn't read just the introduction. I'm on chapter 3. You have a way with words."

"Thanks," Katie said at the half-assed compliment he gave her. They sat in silence, eating and listening to Emma talk.

Katie received her book back from her editor with great reviews. The book was published, and the impact and the support she got from friends and family was more than she could have ever imagined. Katie became a guest on podcasts and spoke about her book and the experience she went through. With each time she told her story, Katie healed her soul with the support of everyone around her. Katie began to look at her life as a whole and change the things she didn't like even more. She forgave herself for things she had done to herself and apologized to and made amends with those she need to.

As Katie's life started to change with her newfound purpose, it seemed to make Taylor stay away even more. It made Taylor "work" more. When Katie would confront Taylor about it, he would say, "I have to work," or "This all would be fixed if we would communicate." Katie was perplexed as she was trying to talk to him; she was trying to be the person Taylor wanted her to be. It seemed no matter what Katie did, it was not good enough. It seemed the more recognition Katie got for her accomplishments, the more Taylor stayed away or picked a fight with her. Katie would always try to de-escalate the situation, but it ended with Taylor leaving.

"Taylor, you are so negative. I am trying to do this for us, our future."

"I can't believe you just said that."

"You are so negative all the time. Why?"

"I'm done talking about this. Screw this shit," Taylor said as he walked out the door and drove off.

Katie was pissed. "This is bullshit. I don't have to deal with this crap." Katie was right; she had ended her divorce before, but she didn't want to give up. She was trying to make it work for Emma and because she did not want to fail at marriage again. Katie was trying to make a marriage work that was never meant to work in the first place. At first, she was worried about parenting all by herself; she thought she couldn't raise Emma alone, but for a few years now, Katie knew if she left, she would be okay. After the years she and Taylor had been together, Katie got used to him being around. She had become accustomed to him being there and being her husband. She knew she deserved better; both of them deserved to be with people who admired them, but they stayed. Maybe they stayed for Emma; maybe they both were scared to start over. Either way, they remained living in separate rooms, living as roommates.

Katie's phone chirped that she had a text message. She looked down, and it was a message from Aaron. She had not heard from Aaron in a while. "Hey, Katie, I haven't heard from you in a while. I was just checking in on you."

Katie stared at the text message. She did not know if she should reply or not. Katie wanted to reply; she wanted Aaron to come and save her from the mess she was in, but Katie knew she had to try. She had to try one more time to know that she did everything she possibly could to save the broken marriage she had been living in the past several years. Katie closed the message without replying to Aaron.

The next few months, Katie tried to work on her marriage. She tried to include Taylor in her podcasts and everything that was going on in her book. She tried to tell Taylor more what she wanted, what she needed, and asked him what he wanted. It always ended in an argument and Taylor leaving the house or staying late at work. Finally, one night, Katie had enough. When she got home late from work, she went to his room and said, "Look, we need to figure out what is going on. We need to either go to counseling, get separated, or get a divorce. We can't keep living like this."

Taylor looked up at Katie with a blank look. "It needs to be one of the last two," he said.

Katie was shocked. "You want to get separated?"

"Yeah, for starters."

"Why? What did I do?" Katie asked.

"It's not you. It's me. I'm just not happy, and you even have said it: if I'm not happy, I can't make you happy, right?" Taylor's smart remark was mocking what Katie had told him many times. Katie always told Taylor he needed to make himself happy because he couldn't make anyone else happy if he wasn't happy.

"I don't get it, Taylor. I work my ass off. I take care of Emma. I clean. I do laundry. I have been faithful to you. What more do I need to do?" Katie asked, getting upset.

Taylor, still with a blank stare, going from looking at Katie to the TV, said, "I've been wanting a divorce for about three years now. There just was never a good time. Just don't want to be married anymore."

Katie stood there in shock. No emotion, as if the past years had meant nothing. He was just done. "I just don't get it, Taylor. Are you talking to other women? I mean, I had a suspicion."

"I've talked to other women, but nothing happened. I couldn't do it. If you had a suspicion, why didn't you say anything?"

"What was I going to do? Confront you so you lied to me?"

Taylor remained silent; he knew Katie was right. If he had cheated on Katie, he would never tell her.

"I don't think I can give Emma up every other weekend and holiday just because you want to leave. I want full custody of Emma, but you can see her whenever you want to."

"Okay," Taylor said. "I don't think I should have to pay child support. And you can have the house. I'm not going to take that from you." The house. Was he serious right now? It was her house. His name wasn't even on the house. Katie knew not to put his name on it.

"Are you sure this is what you want to do? We did have good times," Katie said, trying to think of the last good time they had. It had been a long time ago.

"Yeah," Taylor said.

Katie began to cry, and Taylor said, "Calm down and breathe."

Shocked by Taylor's words, Katie walked out of the room. She had just wasted ten years of her life. Ten years of trying because she thought that was what she was supposed to do. Ten years of no love, no spark for someone who discarded her. She felt used and embarrassed for the way she allowed Taylor to treat her.

Two weeks later, Taylor had Katie sign the divorce papers. The divorce was signed by a judge a week before Christmas. Katie was a single mother now. She was all by herself again.

"But, Katie, you're not telling me what was good about the marriage. You have only told me things that were good when you first started dating years ago," Dr. Spann said. Katie had started therapy with Emma immediately after Taylor said he wanted a divorce.

"I know, but it was ten years, and he didn't give a shit about Emma or me. He just left us like it was no big deal," Katie said, crying.

"You said that you thought about leaving him when Emma got out of school. So what is the difference now or then?"

"Saying and doing are two different things. I didn't want Emma to grow up in a broken home. I wanted her to have her mom and dad."

"It's not uncommon anymore to have the dynamic of divorced parents. Plus, if it wasn't a loving relationship as it seemed not to be, Emma didn't need to see that."

Dr. Spann did make sense, but Katie still felt like a failure. Everything that she worked so hard for, everything she did and her being faithful to Taylor didn't matter. There was nothing Katie could do, and it hurt to not be good enough again. Katie started to feel as if she was living her karma, the karma she deserved for all of the years she had done the same thing— discarding people and never looking back. She felt she deserved it, but ten years was a long time to deal with it. What was she going to do now? She was scared for the first time in a long time.

CHAPTER 16

Katie's phone rang and jolted her from her daydream. She looked down, and it was Emma calling. "Hello, Emma."

"So like we were talking earlier, we really need to talk about this meeting."

"I thought you were in class," Katie said, smiling.

"I was, but I am out for the day. I'm coming over for dinner. What are you cooking?" Emma said.

"Emma, I didn't plan on anything. What do you want?" Katie asked.

"Well, of course, chicken and tater tots."

Katie laughed. When Katie first got divorced, she cooked Emma chicken and tater tots every other night, along with fast food and spaghetti. She tried even though the first year she failed a lot.

"How about I figure out something else? Maybe a little bit healthier," Katie said, smiling.

"Sounds good. See you soon."

Emma was at Katie's house at six. She walked right in and threw her stuff on the ground before slamming the door. "Mom?"

"I'm out here, Emma," Katie said. She was reading before Emma slammed the door.

"Hey, baby girl, how was school?" Katie asked. She was excited to see Emma.

"It was good. I wish I was in more than my basic classes. They are kind of boring," Emma said.

"Well, not many people go to an art high school like you did, Emma. It was one of the great things about moving here, even though you fought it," Katie said, laughing.

"I won't admit it was a good move because I am still mad about leaving my friends, but I do agree I am more advanced than most in my classes."

Katie laughed; she saw a lot of herself in Emma. She was proud of the woman she had become, even though time seemed to slip away to Katie.

Emma changed the subject. "Mom, I want to know what happened. What happened the last time you saw Aaron?"

"Oh, Emma, I told you many times. It was fine. It just didn't work out. We both went our separate ways," Katie said, not wanting to talk about it. Emma knew a lot about her and Aaron, but Katie held the last time she spoke with Aaron close to her.

"Mom, I just don't get it. Everything I know about love, or how I am lacking love in my relationships, is from you and Aaron. It's like a fairy tale, and I just can't imagine you two not being together, seeing each other after ten years."

"Emma, I had you and wanted to move to Florida, and he had the boys. We were just on separate paths, that is all. It wasn't meant to be," Katie explained.

"What happened, Mom? Did you see him again after the last time?" Emma asked.

"No," Katie stated.

"What happened, Mom?" Emma asked sweetly.

Katie knew Emma was not going to stop asking. Katie remembered every detail of the last times she saw Aaron or even talked to him. She closed her eyes and began to tell Emma the story.

———————————————

Katie, two weeks prior, had learned of Taylor wanting a divorce. Her life was in shambles. She was trying to still raise Emma like nothing was wrong and do the podcasts she had agreed to for her book. She put on a happy face and cried behind closed doors. She was seeing a therapist with Emma, as Emma was having a hard time with the divorce. Even though Taylor did not spend much time with her, Emma loved her dad and needed him around. Katie's days were spent comforting Emma and canceling podcasts that she agreed to do. She struggled with not knowing if she could afford to make it on her own and if she could do it as a single parent in law enforcement. Since Taylor had left, he had very little to do with Emma, so Katie sought the friends she did have, to help. Katie hated being vulnerable and asking for help, but she had nothing she could do; she needed the help. As the weeks progressed, Katie realized that she would be okay financially, and she felt as if she was still doing the same things she did before, just without the comfort of Taylor being there.

Katie began to make the house Emma and hers. She painted rooms, she threw out anything that reminded her of Taylor, and she and Emma started new traditions. In the short time since Taylor left, Katie saw a change in Emma. At first, she noticed Emma had grown up, which hurt Katie, knowing that Emma felt she needed to because Katie was hurting. It urged Katie to work harder to heal from Taylor leaving. Second, she saw Emma laughing again and dancing around the living room, acting silly—something Emma had not done for a long time as Taylor would get agitated with Emma and tell her to stop. Katie knew that Taylor leaving was best for both Emma and herself.

Even though Katie knew it was for the best, she still felt hurt, she still was upset, and she pondered why. It was not as if they had a great marriage; they didn't even have a good marriage. Katie started to believe it was her ego, her being divorced. She felt humiliated that she was now a single parent and embarrassed that she had allowed so much to go on during the time she was married. It was more of her actions during the marriage, at what she allowed to go on. Katie needed to start looking at herself and deciding what she wanted.

Katie had the support of her family and friends, but she felt none of them knew her. She felt alone even though she would talk to them about the situation. She felt like no one would understand her; no one did understand the trials and everything in her life. No one except Aaron. Katie picked up her phone and began to text: "I know this is a crazy night, and you are probably with the boys, but I wanted to check on you and see how you were doing." Katie hit send. After she sent the text message, she wished she hadn't. She didn't even know what Aaron was up to. She didn't know if he was dating anyone or if she was going to cause a problem. She didn't know anything about Aaron really for the last ten years.

Almost immediately she received a text message back from Aaron: "It is good to hear from you. How are you doing?"

Katie replied, "I am doing good. How are you and the boys?" Katie was nervous talking to him again, especially how things ended.

"We are okay. The boys are doing good. How are you? Are you married?" Aaron asked Katie. It was like he knew something was wrong and he knew Katie needed him.

"I'm okay. On paper I look like I have things together. I wrote a book and am doing good at my job. Taylor asked me for a divorce. No emotion. He was just done. I feel used."

"Katie, I am sorry. How is Emma handling it?"

"She is doing better than me. I mean, how are you married so long and not have any emotion?"

"You are special, Katie. Don't ever let anyone tell you different. I always felt you were different. You are my friend, and I always want the best for you and Emma."

"I'll remember that and hold you to it. I always think of you more than just a friend."

"Me too. I was thinking of you the other day as well. I miss you, always do."

"I miss you too. We always think alike."

"We have from day one. Katie, those letters you wrote me so long ago meant the world to me. They helped me fight harder knowing I had you to come home to."

"I am so glad they helped."

"I also kept this."

Aaron sent Katie a picture of a picture frame that she had given Aaron years ago.

"I can't believe you kept that," Katie said, shocked.

"I told you I was different. I kept it safe for all of these years," Aaron said. "I still have a folded picture of you I kept in my helmet with me every time I deployed."

With just a few surprise text messages, Katie and Aaron began talking most days. They would not talk for long periods, but they would talk, each hinting that they felt the same way they did years ago about each other. Each enjoyed the thought of the other; you would never have known that it had been ten years since they truly spoke to each other. It was like they picked up where they left off until it got confusing.

"I may have to go overseas for a little while," Aaron said in a message to Katie.

"For how long? Who will watch the boys? Are they going to be okay?" Katie asked.

"The boys will be fine. I don't know much about it yet," Aaron told Katie. "It's a different kind of household."

"Okay, you know I understand," Katie told Aaron. "It's not different. It may be nontraditional, but when have you ever wanted to be traditional, Aaron?"

The two spoke for a few more weeks, not mentioning Aaron leaving again, until one day Katie didn't hear from Aaron. Then the next day and the next. Katie looked at her old text messages, scrolling through them, wondering if she said anything wrong; but she could find nothing. For a month, Katie waited for Aaron to call, text, or email as she did not want to bother him. Katie began to wonder if the whole situation had made Aaron walk away, but Katie just didn't believe it. She just knew he was gone; he was overseas.

> Aaron,
> I kind of miss talking to you. I am guessing you are doing what you love to hate. This past month had me thinking about you. Just tough to look at myself and realize what I knew but didn't want to see. Emma is doing great; I think she is enjoying it being girls' night every night. I want to see you. I know you are probably thousands of miles away, but I just want to be in the same room as you.
> I just wanted to let you know that I was thinking about you. I believe that maybe everything had to fall out of place to fall into place. I don't know if I am right, but I feel like a weight has been lifted off of me and I finally can breathe.
> I want you to know I love you very much. Please come home safe. I will be here when you get back.
>
> Love,
> Katie

Two weeks later, Katie received a message from Aaron.

> Katie,
> I finally had a chance to check my email and I was happy to see an email from you. Yes, I am away right now. I have wanted

to give you space and time that you need.
I would like to see you again, in person.
I've tried to protect the boys from my personal life the best I could. I never wanted to mess up their routine and life. Katie, I love you, always have and always will. Always tell me what you are thinking.
Can't wait to see you again.

Love,
Aaron

Aaron,
Seeing your name in my email made me smile. I can understand protecting the boys from your relationships. I am very protective of Emma too. The last thing I want is for her to get attached to someone for it not to work out. But I am going to say this: by protecting them from your personal life, you are keeping them from all of the love you have to give. The way you love someone is so special, and I hope you share that side of you with them one day.
I miss you, Aaron. Be safe over there.

Always,
Katie

Katie sat back and read Aaron's email again, taking in everything he had said. He wasn't tired of talking to her; he was working. Katie was used to the distance, and she was used to Aaron being overseas. The email sent to her meant more than Aaron knew. Katie knew he was busy and the things he was seeing were horrible. He still took the time to write her an email within the hell he was living at the moment. It gave Katie the momentum to keep pushing toward growth for herself and Emma.

Katie jumped online. She started scrolling through journals until she found one made of leather with a compass on it. To Katie, this symbolized how she and Aaron always seemed to come back to each other. Katie thought, *I can't send him a letter every day. That would seem weird at my age, but I can write him a letter each day he is gone in a journal.* When it arrived, she opened it to the first page.

> Aaron,
> So, I was thinking, since I can't write you every day and we talked about how we wished we would have those letters from a long time ago. Aaron, I love you, and I want you to know I am here. I know what I want and with everything that has gone on, I know where my heart is. It was always with you. I never let anyone get close to me because in a weird way, I knew they could never be you.
> So, in honor of those letters many years ago, and so I don't appear crazy sending you a letter each day, here is your letters in a safe place for you. Here is to the next 30 years, Aaron. I love you and can't wait to see you again.
>
> Love,
> Katie

Katie began doing what she did so many years ago. She wrote Aaron a letter a day and would continue to do so until she knew he was home. Katie and Emma both began to see the future. They began to push toward being happy again. Emma began doing better in school, and Katie went back to doing her podcast episodes to market her book. Katie started writing her second book, and things started to get better. Each month, Katie and Emma started traveling to see family in Florida on Katie's day off. Katie had found a few people she trusted to watch Emma when she couldn't pick her up. Dancing and singing challenges became a must each day at home and in the car. The two were making it together, and both knew they were going to be okay. Every once in a while, Emma would break Katie's heart though. She was an innocent child, but it was still so hard on Katie.

"Mommy, I think you need a boyfriend," Emma said one night as they were sitting on the couch.

Katie looked over at Emma from writing. "Why do you say that?"

"I want you to be happy," Emma said.

"Baby girl, I am happy. I have you, and we are doing good, don't you think?" Katie said, not understanding where the statement had come from.

"I want a new daddy," Emma finally said.

Katie's heart broke. She put down her computer and put her arm around Emma who had started getting tears in her eyes.

"Emma, your daddy is always going to be your daddy. We are doing fine together, and we are making it. If you miss your daddy, text him and tell him you want to see him. You always don't have to have a boyfriend or a man around, Emma. You can do things on your own, and sometimes it is good for you. Relationships are complicated, and there is more that goes into it, baby," Katie explained.

"When will you have a boyfriend again?" Emma asked.

"Why do you want me to have a boyfriend again, Emma? Where is this coming from? You are ten," Katie said. Emma remained quiet. Katie continued, "How about this—it will be me and you for now, and one day if I feel I need to get a boyfriend, me and you will discuss it before I do. Sound like a plan?"

"Okay, Mommy," Emma said, enthused by the answer Katie gave. Emma laid her head on Katie's shoulder, and Katie kissed Emma's forehead.

Katie knew she needed Taylor to see Emma more. Katie had tried to get Taylor to see Emma many times and told him repeatedly that Emma asked about him, but he had only spent time with Emma a handful of times. Katie hoped that as Emma grew, she would realize that Katie was trying to be both a good mom and a good dad for her. Katie wanted to believe that Emma would know that she was doing the best she could. Katie couldn't help but think that she wasn't doing enough due to the questioning of Emma. It made Katie want to push harder for Emma.

Katie pondered if it would even work with the kids. Katie knew Emma wanted siblings, but two boys and a girl. It wasn't about her and Aaron anymore, and she knew both she and Aaron were not going to sacrifice the kids' happiness for themselves. They were both great parents, wanting what was best for them. Both wanted to protect their children from bad relationships and being hurt if it didn't work out. Katie and Aaron were both on the same page about not including the kids until they were sure it would work. They wanted to take things slow, and if they could steal an hour here or there to see each other, it would be worth it. There was no question that the two of them talking had brought happiness and hope back into both of their lives. But Katie wondered if it would be enough. She knew that there was a long road ahead of them with many bumps they would have to overcome. Katie was up for it, but she wasn't sure if Aaron was.

"I want to figure this out, Aaron," Katie whispered. As Katie had promised herself, and as she had promised Aaron many years ago, she wrote him one letter a day.

> Aaron,
> Today was tough. I thought about you a lot. I miss talking to you. You make me feel so safe and it just feels right. Why do things always have to be complicated? I know I am the cause of some of them. I wish I could go back and change some things, but I believe everything happens for a reason and I need to be okay with my decisions.
> I'm scared of you at times. Not physically but for the way you make me feel. I am not

in control with you, if that makes sense. Not that you are controlling, nothing like that, but I would do anything for the way you make me feel. The way that you make me feel just being in a room together. I crave it and I need it.

I miss you and love you very much.

Love Always,
Katie

Aaron,

Today I cannot help but wonder why I haven't heard from you in so long. I know you are over there, but I just don't get it, Aaron. I am trying but it is like you are trying to push me away, and that is fine, but you got to talk to me and tell me. I wish you were here so I could talk to you, so I could tell you everything that is on my mind.

I love you and I really hope to hear from you soon.

Katie only heard from Aaron two times in the months he was overseas, but each time renewed Katie's spirit in the road ahead of them. And then Katie received a message from Aaron: "I am traveling back home. I will be home soon."

"It is good to hear from you. Be safe and see you soon," Katie wrote back. She knew traveling meant within the next week he would be home.

"I am worn out, Katie. Just so tired."

"I know you are, but you are almost home. The boys are going to be so excited to see you. You can get home and relax, well, as much as you can with the boys."

Katie did not hear anything from Aaron after sending the last message. She figured Aaron could not talk or that he finally was getting the sleep he needed. Even though Aaron could not talk, she took out the journal and spoke to Aaron through those words.

Aaron,

I heard from you today. It was so good to hear from you. It made me smile. I can't imagine how excited the boys are going to be to see you. I know you are ready to get home too. We all are ready for you to be home.

I hope when you get home, we can talk more and pick up where we left off. I have missed talking to you. It's like I live for it. There is so many things I want to talk to you about and so many conversations that we never had. I just wish you were here to talk to you about them.

Love,
Katie

About a day later, Katie received a message from Aaron.

"I made it home early this morning."

"Aww, that is awesome. How were the boys?"

"When I got home, I woke them, and they haven't left me. I haven't slept much."

"Oh, I bet it was. Maybe you can get some sleep tonight." Katie thought for a minute and then messaged, "After you get settled in with the boys and work, do you think I can see you?"

"What are you doing tomorrow?" Aaron replied.

Katie was shocked so soon. "Well, I have a meeting tomorrow, but I am good after that."

"Okay, how about I meet you at your house, just to talk? That way if the meeting runs over, we don't have to worry about a time."

"Okay, sounds good. I guess I will see you tomorrow then," Katie said. Katie's nerves were already starting to get to her. After ten years, she would finally see Aaron again. It didn't seem real to Katie. Ten years of not seeing each other, and here they were. They were going to talk for an extended period. What if they didn't have anything to talk about or had awkward silence? What if they didn't feel the same way they had years ago? What if Katie had screwed up any chance of anything between them? She was the reason they weren't together anyway. Aaron was more than ready the last time, and Katie ended up pregnant. Katie couldn't shut off the feeling.

"Hey, I need your address. LOL," Aaron texted.

"I was wondering if you were going to ask me for it, but I figured it would be just as easy to look up. I'm not hard to find. LOL." Katie gave Aaron her address, and the two joked back and forth before saying their goodbyes until the morning.

The next morning, Katie was still nervous. She knew the nerves would be with her until she saw Aaron again. She just wanted them to at least build a friendship like they had years ago. She missed him being in her life, even as a friend.

As Katie thought, she received a text message from Aaron.

"I'm really excited to see you."

"Yeah, me too. A little nervous, but that happens every time before I see you."

As Katie's meeting started, Aaron had not yet arrived. Katie hoped she would be called first to get the meeting over with, but of course she was not. As person after person was called, Katie kept switching her gaze between the computer and the window. As Katie knew she would be one of the next people called, she saw Aaron drive up. *Shit!* Katie thought to herself. She opened the door still listening with one ear to the meeting. She watched as Aaron got out of the car. It was really him, and he was walking right toward her. Katie cracked the door and took a deep breath, still listening to the meeting half-heartedly. When Katie opened the door again, Aaron was standing at the doorway.

"Come in," Katie managed to get out.

The two stood facing each other. Katie could only stare; she was frozen and was just looking at Aaron. She could not believe that he was standing in front of her after ten years. After what felt like an eternity, Aaron finally said, "I need a hug."

Katie smiled and gave Aaron a hug. Aaron lifted Katie up before putting her back down. Katie pulled away, remembering her meeting.

"My meeting is almost over. Do you want to sit down?" Katie said. Her nerves were getting the best of her. She sat down at the computer, trying to get her thoughts together and get her head in the meeting. Katie took a deep breath and let it out where Aaron could not see it, as she was facing her computer.

Katie turned to look at Aaron. She could not believe that he was sitting on her couch. "How was the drive?" Katie asked.

"It was good. Not too long," Aaron said, smiling. Katie smiled back. "I actually have a meeting I need to go to at the base. It seems that everyone is wanting to do meetings today."

"Katie, you got an update?" Katie heard from the computer.

Katie stumbled through her updates, messing up names and having her supervisor question what she was saying. Katie felt like an idiot; it was rare for her not to be on her game. One of the other supervisors whom Katie knew messaged her.

"Are you okay? Do I need to take over?"

"I am good. I'm going to be busy for a few. Cover for me." Katie sent a coffee emoji to him. The other supervisor briefly knew about Katie and Aaron's history, and he knew that they were going to have coffee soon. "I got you," he messaged back.

Katie turned back to Aaron. "I'm sorry. It will be over soon."

Aaron just smiled. "It's okay."

Once the meeting concluded, Katie clicked out of the meeting, turning back to Aaron. She smiled. "Hi."

Aaron smiled. "I need to get another hug."

Katie leaned over and hugged Aaron's neck tightly. He wrapped her arms around Katie. The two embraced for what felt like ten minutes. Once they pulled back, Katie asked how he and the boys were doing. She asked about the meeting he had. It was small talk as Katie was still trying to calm her nerves from seeing Aaron after so long. Aaron seemed happy; he seemed like he was happy to be there with Katie.

"I can't believe you are here," Katie said. Aaron looked at Katie and grabbed her to hug her again. Katie wrapped her hands around Aaron's neck and placed her hands in his hair.

"I missed this," Aaron said, tightly wrapping his arms around Katie.

"Me too," Katie said as she buried her head into Aaron's neck and closed her eyes. She could feel Aaron's heart beating; it was pounding so loud and fast. The pounding and being so close to Aaron made Katie feel so safe. When Aaron started to play with Katie's hair, all the nerves that Katie felt started to melt away. The two sat in silence just holding on to each other, something they had not done in decades. There were no words spoken, just their hearts speaking to each other. It felt right, it felt comforting, and it felt the furthest from complicated as they both worried about. It was Katie and Aaron; it would always be Katie and Aaron. Somehow, being together made life always make sense.

As the two pulled away from each other, Aaron slid his hand out of Katie's hair and to her face. Their faces met, and they paused, touching their foreheads together. Katie could feel her heart beating, and she was breathing heavy. She and Aaron leaned in, kissing each other's lips. Katie grabbed on to Aaron as they kissed. Katie pulled away from one of the many kisses they had shared.

"You scare me," Katie whispered.

"You scare me too," Aaron said.

"I needed to go through what I went through this last time. It was a lesson," Katie said.

Aaron looked at Katie. "Oh yeah?"

"Yeah," Katie said.

Katie grabbed Aaron's face and kissed him again.

Katie's phone interrupted the teenage make-out session that they had been in.

"Sorry, I have to get that," Katie said.

"Go ahead. It's okay," Aaron said.

"Hello. No, the body is being taken up on Wednesday for autopsy. Yeah. No warrants are being taken today." Katie paused for the person on the phone. "Yeah, I can let you know. Okay, thanks."

Katie turned to Aaron. "I'm sorry."

Aaron smiled. "I understand."

"I want to get out, but it is hard to find anything around here making what I make."

"I understand that. How much longer do you have?" Aaron questioned.

"I have another year and a half before I can. I want to write. I want to get back to Florida. What is your plans?"

"I want to go overseas one more time and do something else." As Aaron spoke, Katie's heart dropped at his next comment. "The boys and I have been talking about moving to Alaska. We say it will be a new adventure."

"Alaska?"

"Yeah, we liked it up there, and it is so pretty there."

"Isn't it like dark there all the time and cold?"

Aaron laughed. "Yes, but you know I like the cold. It's peaceful there."

"I get it," Katie said, crushed. "How soon are you going to do that?"

"Well, the boys are going to visit her parents this summer. I figured I would go overseas then. The plan was to get through this school year, and then we would see."

"Oh, I got you," Katie said before changing the subject.

Katie and Aaron spoke for another hour about life and the trials they both had faced. Both comforted each other as they spoke about the hardships they had faced alone. They both spoke about how the hardships had taken a toll on them physically and mentally. Both spoke about just wanting peace for who they had become as people.

"Oh dang, Katie, I got to go. I'm going to be late for the meeting if I don't," Aaron said, surprised at how much time had passed. It felt like Aaron had just got there, but it had already been two hours.

"Let me get this meeting done, and I will come back before I go home," Aaron said.

"Okay, that will be good," Katie said as they walked to the door.

Aaron opened the door, hugged Katie, and kissed her one last time. "See you in a few."

"Okay," Katie said, standing at the door watching Aaron walk away. Katie did not want Aaron to go. As Aaron was walking away, he turned to look at Katie again. His face looked sad as he looked back at Katie. Katie looked at Aaron with a blank stare. Aaron turned around and walked away. Katie watched as Aaron got into his car and pulled away. Katie walked back inside and sat down on the couch. It seemed like a dream to her, a dream that was too fast. At least she would be able to see Aaron again before he went back home. As time passed, it got closer and closer to time that Aaron had to leave to go and pick up his boys. Katie realized she would not be able to see Aaron before he left.

"The meeting ran late. I got to get the boys."

Katie could tell when Aaron was anxious, and this was one of those times.

"Do you have someone that can go get them until you get there? Drive safe."

"Yes. I don't like doing this to them when I told them I would pick them up."

"I know. I get it, but I know they will understand."

"Yes, but I don't like doing it to them."

"Please be safe getting home. It was good to see you today."

It was several hours before Katie heard from Aaron again.

"Would you like to talk tomorrow?"

"Yeah, sure, that would be great," Katie messaged.

"I will message you in the morning to see what is going on."

"Okay, sounds good."

Katie was with Emma doing schoolwork when Aaron messaged. Katie knew how stressful it was when her plans changed unexpectedly. She understood Aaron's anxiety and disappointment for letting the boys down. She had experienced it several times with Emma. That was one of the rough parts about her job—things could change in a moment's notice.

Katie waited the next morning for Aaron to call, but he messaged later that morning.

"Sorry, I was with my aunt, and time just got away from us."

"That's okay," Katie said. "How is she doing?"

"She is doing good. My uncle isn't doing very well."

"Dang, I'm sorry to hear that."

"It is that time in our life when the old start to pass on."

"It doesn't make it any easier though," Katie texted.

"No, it doesn't, but that's just how it works. I was thinking of taking her with us to Alaska."

"Don't take this the wrong way, but aren't you running away doing that?"

"Maybe partially, but we really like it up there."

"You got to face everything you are going through, Aaron. You are wandering, trying to fix the problem. The boys don't care where you live. They just want to have you home with them, Aaron."

Katie waited for a reply from Aaron, but he never messaged again. The next day, Katie messaged Aaron, "If what I said to you yesterday hurt you, I did not mean for it to. I am sorry. I guess it is me being selfish. I am not ready to let you go this time."

Aaron did not reply. Katie knew that Aaron was going to Texas; maybe he couldn't talk. A week turned into two weeks, which turned into three weeks. Katie messaged Aaron again in hopes that he would message her back. "I am thinking about you. What you are going through doesn't scare me. What scares me is you not being around forever. I love you very much."

Katie heard nothing. A month then turned into a month and a half. Katie tried two more times to contact Aaron but received no reply.

Katie could not imagine what she had done wrong. She had reached the point where she knew she had to let Aaron go. She knew if he wanted to, he would message her, like he always did when she would surprise him with a message or an email after a period. Katie cried, as she felt this was the time they were going to make it work. She felt she had waited too long. Aaron was moving to Alaska, and there was nothing she could do about it. She had to let him go, to be happy and to find peace in Alaska. Aaron had made up his mind, and no matter how strong their feelings were when they were together, both Katie and Aaron knew distance and not talking could make the living without each other doable. It just hurt; it broke Katie's spirit and shattered the hope she had.

Katie went over the day she and Aaron spent together a thousand times. She analyzed every detail of it and just could not understand what happened. Katie knew guys; she knew them from working with them for so long and in her own relationships. She knew that what she felt the day that she and Aaron shared couldn't be faked. She knew Aaron felt it too. It was the words not spoken, the way that they looked at each other. Then Katie would go back to when Aaron was leaving, the look on his face, as if he knew it would be a while before he saw her again. His look haunted Katie since Aaron had stopped communicating with her.

Katie tried; she tried to be positive about not messaging Aaron. She tried to tell herself, *This is what Aaron needs. He needs his time and space. He will come back again. We always come back together.* Katie started thinking, *Is there someone else in the picture?* But then she would question why Aaron had said different things alluding to it being just him and the boys. Katie thought that it was a lot to process. Five months earlier, she had just got a divorce and was talking to Aaron about it. Maybe he was worried she saw him as a rebound, but that wasn't the case for Katie. Other men had asked her out, but she knew what was right in her heart. Her heart belonged to Aaron and no one else; it always had and always would.

Katie found solace in the journal that she had kept for the past five months.

Aaron,

Today I looked at your picture and cried. I know I got to let you go. I know right now is not the time and I know that if we are supposed to be together, we will find each other again. I just don't know what to do. My mind says let it go and keep moving on but something inside me keeps telling me to hang on. Something keeps telling me don't give up. It's like you are talking to me in my quiet moments when I am thinking of you.

I listen to the radio or your playlist and I just am brought back to all the memories. Memories that I never want to forget. I want more memories though; I want to have so many memories in one day I can't go through them all. I guess, I just don't want to go another year or 10 years where we don't talk anymore. I don't want to be like that anymore, but I wonder if I am crazy to keep believing you are coming back.

I know I have to come to terms with you moving. I know I have to be okay with it, but it is just so hard. I hope you are growing, and I hope that you are happy. I never want anything more than you to be happy, even if I am not with you. Be happy, Aaron, and find your peace. I love you more than you know.

Always,
Katie

Katie had written so many entries into the journal. Some were angry, most were their memories or thoughts, but a lot were her dreams for the future. Things she thought about when she sat in silence; sometimes she even dreamed about them. Katie had started dreaming about future events, and the dreams seemed so real to her. She thought that she would give the journal to Aaron the next time she saw him, but the next time never came for Katie. So instead, it became a journal of her thoughts of Aaron, written to him to document her thoughts during the week of him.

> Aaron,
> I had a dream last night of you. It wasn't about past events this time; it was future things. It felt so real, and I wish the dream never ended. Do you dream about us? Do you dream about future events or just the past?
> I've stopped writing every day and have started writing on the days that are the worst. I miss talking to you. I feel like a crazy person. I may never be able to give you this journal now with all of my thoughts in it. You did say you wanted to know what I was thinking. I guess this is a good way of documenting it, not to forget. LOL. It is getting easier. God, I just miss talking to you. I say if I could only see you one more time, but that will never be enough, Aaron. I would want more.
> I hope you are safe wherever you are.
>
> Always,
> Katie

Week after week Katie continued to pour her thoughts into the journal, and week after week that passed, she did not hear from Aaron.

It was like he disappeared, and Katie did not know what happened. She thought it was her fate and karma for all of the things she did in her past. Katie was okay with getting the karma she deserved but thought at times it was excessive. The absence of Aaron had forced Katie to throw herself even more into obviously Emma and her work, but Katie had the urge to write another book. One night as she thought about the last months, she opened her computer and titled a Word document "Title Unknown," then she wrote:

> Katie looked out into the ocean as the
> waves crashed into the sand . . .

As much as she wanted to do life with Aaron, Katie knew she had to do things her own way. She deserved to be truly happy, and Emma deserved to have the best life Katie could give her. It was up to her, and she had to stay focused on her goals. She deserved it.

CHAPTER 17

"So you haven't heard from him since?" Emma asked in shock.

"No, I haven't," Katie replied, looking down.

"No emails, no text messages, no phone calls?" Emma continued to ask.

"No, I haven't heard from him. I would like to think he was happy and at peace wherever he was at in life. I believe he had made the decision to move to Alaska, and he wanted to do everything he could for the boys to be happy."

"I just don't believe that. I mean, I know that is what you are telling me, but something happened. I mean, it was all there." Emma sounded confused.

"I know, and at times I would think about it. It would drive me crazy. So crazy I thought I needed to be medicated. Both Aaron and I knew we couldn't keep talking to each other and seeing each other. We had you kids to think about and what was best for you guys."

"So you two were miserable for us. Thanks, Mom," Emma said sarcastically.

Katie laughed. "Emma, I was not miserable, and I am sure Aaron wasn't either. We both have been through a lot in our life, and our biggest goal was to make sure that you guys didn't have the same life we had. We wanted you to be protected from everything we weren't. We wanted you all to be aware of the evil in the world, but we didn't want you to have to be in the middle of it, if we could help it. We just love you all so much," Katie explained to Emma.

"So you were okay being a single parent for all these years?" Emma questioned.

"Yes, I think both Aaron and I knew deep down, we had to give each other up to give to you guys everything. In our heart, we knew that we would always find each other again. One day," Katie said, smiling.

"That's a long fucking one day!" Emma said.

"EMMA."

"I'm an adult, Mom. You cussed like a sailor when I was growing up," Emma said.

"Yeah, and I told you to be better than me. As I was saying, being a single parent didn't bother me. My heart was always with Aaron. I had tried marriage more times than I should have. My heart was always with Aaron and still is. I just knew it would be best to do everything I possibly could to make your life perfect. Being single isn't a bad thing, Emma, when your heart is already full. I already had my rock star, and I was already raising her. As much as we want to believe, life is not a fairy tale. Sometimes no matter how much love there is, it just doesn't make it. Emma, you know this."

"I know, but why couldn't you guys do it together? I mean, I always wanted a sibling anyway."

"Your spoiled ass wouldn't have lasted two days with siblings. Hell, I just got you out of my bed."

"Haha. I stopped sleeping in your bed it sounds like soon after you and Aaron stopped talking. When did you decide to move to Florida, and how did you choose Ponte Vedra?" Emma questioned.

Katie smiled. "Well, I had already been looking at different places in St. Augustine and Palm Coast."

"Again, how did we get here, and when did you decide for sure we were going to move?" Emma asked, raising her eyebrow.

Katie looked out to the water and began to tell Emma the story of how they ended up in Ponte Vedra.

Katie had started looking at houses and told Emma about it, but she was specifically looking for houses in St. Augustine and Palm Coast. She had a realtor sending her daily listings of new houses on the market. While buying a house wasn't something that was going to happen in the near future, Katie liked getting an idea of how much a house would cost so she could save up for when that time came.

When Aaron came back into the picture and Katie talked about moving back to the beach, Aaron wanted to know where she planned to move. Katie told him the areas she was considering and the listings she was reviewing.

"I know my family lives on the Gulf Coast, but I don't know. I just really like the area. I want to live by the beach, but that doesn't mean I want it so busy. I just don't know if I could get used to the traffic and so many people. Plus I want Emma to enjoy the town we live in, and she loves St. Augustine. The cost of living isn't horrible there either. More than here but not as bad as other places I've seen in Florida. There isn't anything for me here anymore. I thought I was always going back to Florida. Hell, you know that, and here I am years later, the only one in my family left here. It is time. I just got to talk Emma into it."

"When do you think you are going to move?" Aaron asked Katie.

"I don't know. I know I am here another year and a half. I started looking at jobs, but I haven't found anything that pays what I get paid here, and obviously, the cost of living is higher down there. I would love for my book to take off and just write. I would love just to write and take care of Emma and make my own schedule around her."

Aaron smiled. "Check Ponte Vedra."

"Really," Katie said.

"Yeah, you would like it there. What are you going to do with this house? Sell it and put the money down on another house?" Aaron asked.

"Probably. There is nothing left for me here, but this house has a lot of memories in it. My dad and I built this house together. I raised Emma in this house. Just not sure yet."

"You will get there, Katie. I know you will," Aaron said, smiling.

Katie smiled. "Thanks."

After Aaron and Katie stopped talking, Katie began to write her second book. Within two months, she had it completed. She decided to publish her second book the same way she published her first book. She did everything herself, hiring those she needed to put the final touches on it. Katie started to get nervous publishing her first fiction book. She thought it was perfect but could not gauge whether anyone would want to read a story of love. A story of love that was the skeleton of what Aaron and Katie had gone through themselves. A story of falling in love as kids and as adults, not letting each other go. No matter how much time passed, no matter what obstacles were in the way, they made it. With thoughts of Emma, the boys, and Aaron in her mind, Katie took a deep breath and hit publish.

The next few months were a whirlwind of emotions for Katie. Katie, an average single mom, became popular in contemporary romance. Her first fiction book was selling, and selling a lot, more than Katie could have ever imagined. People who read it were deeply touched by the love Katie described in it and cheered "Molly" and "Liam" to finally get it right. Katie, of course, had them end up together after years of misfortunes. She was not a *New York Times* best seller, but the book had helped Katie afford what she always wanted. For the first time, Katie felt like her purpose was to bring words to people. Words that others could resonate with and others could understand. She did it first with book number one, and now she was doing it again with a story similar to her and Aaron's story.

The next year flew by for Katie. She had the time she needed to leave the job she was currently at, at any point. Katie had a salary that would allow her to live worry free in Florida, and she did not need to look for a job that paid little and took more time away from Emma. Katie would take Emma down to Florida every chance she got and try to talk her into moving to Florida. One day, Emma said, "Mommy, I want to move to Florida." Katie started looking for a house or condo endlessly until she found the perfect one in Ponte Vedra.

Every fear in Katie's body was keeping her from moving forward. Her anxiety was so bad, and at times it was debilitating. One step at a time, Katie did it. She put her house on the market and started packing up her things. She was excited to finally move back to Florida, back to where she was born and back to where she always thought she belonged. Each item she packed had a memory of the now thirty years she had lived in the house. With each new box, Katie thought about all the memories she had made in the house. She smiled and she cried as the house began to be an empty shell. As the weeks passed, Katie looked around the house, the door that Emma was allowed to draw and paint on, Emma's growth chart on the door, and the dints and scratch marks on the walls from Emma running into things with her scooter or her roller blades.

Katie walked to Emma's room. As she opened the door, the pink walls with purple polka dots were showing. Katie walked in and sat on the bed, looking at the mess she had asked Emma to clean up but hadn't yet. Katie smiled looking around the room. She thought about how much joy Emma had brought to her life since the day she was born. Emma had saved Katie more than she knew. Since Taylor left, they had grown together in love and determination. Taylor moved away for work over a year early, and Emma got a text message every so often from him. Although Emma struggled with it for a long time, she got used to it and gained a better understanding of it. This move was a new start for both of them. Emma had grown into such a loving and sweet child. Katie could only be proud of her as a daughter and the young lady she had become. Katie smiled, standing up and walking to the door before closing it.

Katie then walked to the living room and sat down on the couch. She looked around the bare living room. All of the pictures were packed away, and all that were left were the TV and the couch—the same couch that Katie had the last time she saw Aaron. Katie leaned her head back and got lost in her thoughts. Aaron would not know where she lived again. Aaron had known every house she had lived in, and she was moving again. So many times, Katie hoped that Aaron would just show up unannounced and tell her that he couldn't live without her. She hoped each time she came over the hill going down to her house that Aaron's car would be in the driveway waiting for her. So many days she sat on the front porch listening to music and thinking about the few memories that they had together here. She could remember the day so clearly even though it had been over a year. She still missed Aaron and thought about him daily. She wanted to believe that somehow, they were still connected.

Katie always believed everything happened for a reason, and she still did to this day. She believed that she had to do it on her own. She had to raise Emma and build the life she wanted. It was her last dream, and unfortunately, Aaron could not come along with her. Katie had to pick new dreams now, and she was picking harder dreams; she believed she could do anything.

Katie looked over to where Aaron had sat over a year ago. She could still see him sitting there with a smile and those gorgeous blue eyes staring back at her. She leaned her head back and closed her eyes again. She whispered, "I did it, Aaron. I'm moving back to Florida. I did everything I said I was going to." Tears started to form in Katie's eyes as she whispered, "I am still waiting for you like I told you I would. Come back, love."

Katie wondered if Aaron even knew—if he knew that Katie had done everything she said she was going to do. She wondered if Aaron had read her books or even knew about them. Most of all, she wondered if he knew she did it all for Emma, the boys, and him. They were all the driving force behind all of the hours, the late nights, and the struggles. They all were the reason Katie pushed so hard. Not only was she making a better life for Emma, she was wanting to make a better life for Aaron and the boys too.

A little over a month later, Katie was standing in the doorway of the now-empty house she had called home. The only thing left in the house was the couch that Katie had. Katie was leaving it behind with the memories she had in the house with Aaron. It was her way of letting go of the memories to make more in the future. Teary eyed, Katie took a deep breath and closed the door for the last time. As she drove away from the house, she looked in the rearview mirror. Emma was sitting up from her seat, on her knees, looking back as well. Tears started to form as Katie looked back at the house, but they were hidden by her sunglasses.

"Mommy, I am going to miss our house," Emma said.

Clearing her throat, Katie said, "I know, baby girl, but we are going on a new adventure." The phrase was something Aaron had said a year earlier.

"Do you think I will make new friends?" Emma said worriedly.

"Of course, everyone is going to love you, girl," Katie said as she turned the corner. The house she thought she would own forever now was just a memory.

———————————————

"Wait," Emma said. "You are telling me we moved here because Aaron, a guy I have never met, said to check for houses here."

Katie started laughing. "Yes, and you enjoyed growing up here, didn't you?"

"Yes, but, Mom, you moved here with hopes that he would come back here to find you, didn't you?"

"No, Emma, I knew Aaron would find me if he wanted to. I never changed my number. I couldn't. I moved here because in some way, I felt close to him here. Even though he wasn't here, it was something we talked about, and in a strange way, I felt like he was a part of it," Katie said.

"But you just said you left the couch at the house. I loved that couch."

Katie laughed. "We got another couch that you screwed up just as much as that couch." Emma glared at Katie. Katie continued, smiling, "Well, you and the dogs."

"I can't believe you are not seeing this, Mom," Emma said, shocked.

"See what, Emma?" Katie asked, confused.

"Mom, you have stayed single for eight years. You moved to Ponte Vedra, Florida, a city that you two have spoken about. You did everything that you told Aaron you wanted to do," Emma said sternly.

"Yeah, pretty much, but I did it for you and I, Emma. To be totally honest though, Aaron and the boys were a little push too and always in the back of my mind. If Aaron ever did come back, I didn't want to make him or the boys suffer. I wanted to have my own career, our own life. That's the stubborn in me."

"I know, and I am grateful I am here and have done the things I have done, but don't you think there is going to be more to this than you think?"

"No, Emma, I don't. Let's just see what tomorrow brings."

Emma, sensing that Katie didn't want to talk about it anymore, finally said, "Okay, but I am staying tonight so I can talk to you some more about this tomorrow."

"Christ, I can't wait for tomorrow to come because I do believe you have more anxiety than I do with the situation."

Katie and Emma stayed up, sitting out on the porch watching the waves crash for a few hours. Katie enjoyed talking to Emma about all of her hopes and dreams. Dreams so big that they seemed impossible to achieve. Katie reaching her dreams gave hope to Emma on those days when Emma thought her dreams were too big. It gave Katie comfort knowing that she had done everything that she possibly could for Emma. She had done her job as a parent. As a single mom, she raised an amazing child, and she did it all on her own. Katie had a sense of pride in it knowing how differently her life could have been depending on her choices.

"The sky is so clear tonight," Emma said, looking up into the night sky.

Katie looked up. "Yeah, it is."

As the two looked, they saw a shooting star.

Emma smiled. "Look, it's a shooting star! Make a wish." Both were quiet for a moment until Emma finally said, "I bet I know what you wished for."

"Oh, Emma," Katie said, getting up from her chair. "I am going to bed. Are you coming?"

"Yeah, I will in a minute."

"Okay, baby girl. See you in the morning. Love you," Katie said before turning around and walking to her room.

"Night, Mom, love you too." Emma watched as Katie walked inside and walked into her room. Secretly Emma had wished for her mom to find the closure she needed and a fairy-tale ending in her life.

Katie walked into her room and closed her door. She sat down at the armoire in her room and looked in the mirror. As she brushed her hair, she looked at herself. She had aged in the last eight years. She had accomplished everything that she wanted to, but she still didn't have one thing. She didn't have Aaron, and her heart ached. Katie set down her brush and looked over at Oliver, her dog, that was watching her. "Well, Oliver, this is as good as it is going to get." Oliver wagged his tail and got up from where he was lying when Katie got into bed.

Katie closed her eyes, and thoughts of Aaron came to her mind. Tomorrow she would have the answers she had been needing for so long. Maybe she would have a better understanding. An image of Aaron dressed in his military uniform flashed into her mind. It was the picture Katie had traced with her fingers many times and whispered to. The image was burned in her mind. It was not long before Katie was fast asleep.

Chapter 18

Katie's heart was racing. She was so nervous after all these years. To relive all of the memories, to feel her heart actually feel something again. Something that she had not felt in eight years. Katie took a breath and opened the door to the coffee shop where they agreed to meet.

As she looked around, she saw him sitting in a booth toward the back of the room. As she walked over, he looked up, smiled, and stood up to greet her.

"Ms. Katie?" Katie nodded, smiling. "It's really good to meet you," he said, leaning over to hug her.

"Sam, it's really good to see you again. Please call me Katie. Where is John?"

"He couldn't come. He was not ready," Sam said, looking down.

"Well, that is understandable. He is only eighteen," Katie replied.

"Yeah, he's still a free spirit per se, kind of does his own thing."

Katie laughed. "I know someone else that was just like him."

Sam half smiled and looked down.

"It was really good to hear from you, Sam. I know the first time you met me was at the funeral. I know it took a lot to reach out to me," Katie said, changing the subject.

"It did. I did not know if the interaction would be taken well," Sam said. As Sam spoke, Katie thought he articulated his words just like Aaron.

"Sam, I love you boys, and you are a piece of Aaron. I know more about you than you know. Aaron and I would talk about you boys and Emma often."

"John and I never knew. We really didn't know if Dad mentioned us to you."

"Of course he did. I heard about your extracurricular activities, how you were doing in school, and of course your fishing trips. I never got to meet you, but I met John when he was an infant. Did you know that?"

"No, I didn't know that," Sam said.

"Your dad loved you boys so much and was proud of you both. He never loved anything more. You were his world, especially when things got bad." She spoke.

"We knew a little about you. We were still kind of young. We knew that you were good friends from a long time ago. Even back then, we knew that there was something more there. We didn't know how much until later on. You were a big part of his life for many years."

Katie had tears forming in her eyes. "He did tell you about me. I didn't think you guys even knew who I was when I introduced myself to you. I'm glad he did."

"Yes." Sam smiled. "He told us that you told him the way he loved someone was special."

Katie smiled. "I did tell him that many years ago. Sam, what happened? I know he was going to deploy one more time. After that, you guys were moving to Alaska to live."

Sam looked down. "The individuals they were deployed with heard that there was a family left in a village alone. Dad and the other individuals went to go help them. I know they got them out of the village, but after that, they really don't know. He didn't survive it, Ms. Katie."

Katie just looked down at the tissue she had in her hand, pulling it apart.

"Ms. Katie, we weren't moving to Alaska."

Katie looked up at Sam. "What do you mean you weren't moving to Alaska?"

"Dad, John, and I all made the decision when Dad got back, we were going to move to a different place in Florida and start what Dad called a new adventure."

Katie's heart dropped, and tears began to stream down her face.

Sam said, "I don't know why he changed his mind, but, Ms. Katie, I am sure it had something to do with you. We didn't care where we move. We were just happy that Dad was going to be home more to see him. He didn't tell you?"

Katie, still shaken, said, "No, I didn't know." Katie's heart was breaking even more than the day that she learned of Aaron's death.

"I always figured you knew."

"No, I didn't know, Sam. After we saw each other the last time, I decided to let him go and find what he needed. I just wanted him to be happy and at peace. I knew if he wanted to, he would find me again."

"You waited for him?" Sam asked with a surprised look on his face.

"Yes, I did. I made a lot of mistakes in my life, but one thing I knew, when or if he did come back, I would be here."

"You loved him that much? Seems lonely."

"Yes, I did wait. Now, I did live my life with Emma, and we made a lot of memories. I just put relationships in the back of my mind and excelled in my career and let Emma have the best life I could give her. All my love poured into her. It wasn't lonely. I had her and plenty of things in my life not to think about it."

"Oh, thank you for loving my dad the way you did. I want to know all about my dad. How long did you know him?"

Katie laughed. "I met your dad when I was fifteen years old."

Sam smiled. "How old was my dad?"

"Hmm, he was either sixteen or seventeen at the time. We were about a year apart."

Katie and Sam talked about Aaron. They talked about funny times Aaron and Katie shared through the years. Sam seemed to enjoy knowing more about his dad as a teenager and being in his twenties. Katie enjoyed hearing about Aaron as a dad. Katie never got to experience Aaron as a dad. Listening to Sam's stories, Katie was right—Aaron was a wonderful dad who lived for the boys. Katie looked down at her watch.

"I really have to be going, Sam. You and I talked like your dad and I did. We could talk for hours and lose track of time," Katie said.

"Before you go, Ms. Katie, I wanted to give you something. We found these in my dad's things, and I thought you might want them."

Katie looked as Sam pull out a crumpled-up picture and a picture frame. He slid it across the table. Katie's heart fluttered.

"He had both of these with him when it happened. The picture was in his helmet, and the picture frame was in one of his duffel bags. Isn't that you, Ms. Katie?"

Katie's eyes began to tear up again. She picked up the picture and looked at it. "Yes, I gave your dad that picture almost forty years ago. It was one of my high school senior pictures. He told me he carried it in his helmet every time he deployed. The picture frame I sent in one of the care packages I sent him fortyish years ago too. I knew he had kept it for thirty years. I didn't know he still had it."

"He did. It was with him, Ms. Katie," Sam said. "There is something else." Sam slid an envelope across the table toward her. The envelope had "Katie" written on it in Aaron's handwriting.

"I didn't open it, but I am guessing it is a letter for you. It makes sense now after you telling me about the letters you two wrote to each other over the years."

Katie picked up the envelope on the table. "Thank you, Sam." Katie paused. "Not that it matters, but where were you guys going to move to?"

"Huh, Ponte Vedra, St. Augustine, or Palm Coast. We were going to visit them when he got back and decide. Thank you again, Ms. Katie, for coming. This has helped me," Sam said.

Katie looked up from the envelope and smiled. "Yes, of course. It was good to see you again, Sam. It has helped me too. You are always a part of Aaron, and you can call me anytime."

"Thank you, Ms. Katie."

Katie walked out of the coffee shop clutching the picture frame in her arms. She got back in her car and looked at the picture frame before placing it down on the seat next to her. She picked up the crumpled picture that was so tattered you could barely see the picture of her remaining on it. She stared at it thinking about how many deployments and how many times Aaron probably looked at the picture. Katie placed the picture on the same seat that she had placed the picture frame on. She grabbed the envelope. "Katie" was written on the front. She ran her fingers over Aaron's writing on the envelope. She felt as if Aaron knew he had to write everything down in a letter, as if he knew he may never come home. Katie opened the envelope.

Katie,

If you are reading this, I have messed up pretty bad. I hope that you will never read this letter and that we are living somewhere together with Emma and the boys. But if you are, I'm so sorry, Katie, that I didn't make it back home this time. Know I fought my hardest to get home to all of you.

My Katie, from the first time we met, I knew you would change my life. The first time you laid your head in my lap, me running my fingers through your hair, just talking, I knew my heart would never be the same. You were always special to me, and don't let anyone ever tell you different.

Those letters you wrote me all those years ago meant so much to me. It made me fight harder knowing that someone cared about me so much. I wanted to give you the world, Katie, but we always seemed to fall short. Many times, we tried to push each other away, but we always came back to each other, like soulmates, as you always would say.

What I wouldn't give to be curled up with you one last time. Just to feel you next to me and talk the night away like we did when we were kids. Those are memories I cherish.

I always carried you in my heart and mind, Katie. No matter how much time passed, I always missed and loved you. I know I loved you until my last breath in this life, and I will love you in the next. Live, Katie, I am always with you.

I love you, Katie,
Aaron

PS. I did read your books. It doesn't surprise me how much they are loved. The one *Whispered Promises* seems kind of familiar. ;) I loved both of them.

Katie laid down the letter and stared off at nothing. Aaron was coming back to her. They were going to do the rest of their lives together when he got home. Sam had given Katie what she needed, closure on what happened, and Aaron gave closure to Katie that he was coming home to her. Katie wiped the tears from her eyes and whispered, "Thank you for this, Aaron. God, I miss you so much every day."

CHAPTER 19

Katie sat up straight in her bed. She was breathing hard and sweating. She looked around, and there was light outside. She looked around, trying to get her bearings and think, *It was a dream. It was just a dream. Everything is fine.* Katie started breathing deeply to calm her heart down, which was racing. She slid to the side of her bed, placing her head in her hands. *What the hell is wrong with me?* she thought. *How could I even dream of such a thing?* Katie kept telling herself, *It was a dream. It was a dream, Katie, calm down. Aaron is fine.*

Katie stood up and walked to the kitchen where Emma was already up eating breakfast and watching something on her phone. Katie walked to the coffeepot and poured a cup of coffee. Emma looked up from her phone.

"What the hell happened to you?" Emma said after taking a double look at Katie.

"Emma, I'm old. We all look like this in the morning, but I had a nightmare last night. I can't wait to get this over with. Maybe I'll sleep at night peacefully," Katie said, smiling.

"I think it is nerves, and whether you admit it or not, you want this to work out. You want the fairy tale you write about in your books," Emma said, smiling.

"Emma, fairy tales aren't real. I thought I taught you better," Katie said, walking back to her room to take a shower and get ready to meet Aaron.

"I think you do believe!" Emma yelled to Katie as she walked down the hallway.

Katie began to get ready for her coffee meeting with Aaron. All the memories and all of the emotions that went along with them came flooding back to her. Katie's nerves began to get the best of her. It always happened when she knew she was going to see Aaron. Katie always heard it was bad to get so nervous to see someone, that the body was trying to tell someone something when they got like that. To Katie, it was her way of confirming that Aaron was the one for her. Without fail, Katie's nerves would disappear with one hug, one touch, or one kiss from him. Aaron did this to Katie the first day they met and every time they saw each other through the years. It was the reason Katie always held on to one day with Aaron. There was always something about him, and as Katie thought about her life and where she was at now, she believed that everything happened for a reason, and she was here at this point meeting Aaron for yet another reason that she really didn't understand. Katie stopped questioning why years ago; she thought it was a question she would never get answered, but she believed she had to learn a lot of lessons before she could be at the point she was now in her life.

Katie looked in the mirror, her now fifty-something face. She hardly recognized the person who was staring back at her. She could not understand how fast the time went by, and yet it seemed like it was last week that she met Aaron for the first time. It was hard to believe that here they were in their fifties already. Katie always believed that she and Aaron would grow old together, they would have kids together, they would be married, but it never happened. Life always pulled the two of them apart after seeing each other, but they always came back to each other. Neither was willing to give up on the other or give up on the hope of one day. Emma was right, Katie did believe in fairy tales. Aaron's love was the reason why she knew there was love that lasted lifetimes. Deep down, Katie always held on to hope that Aaron would come back one day. She never told anyone, but secretly she whispered it to herself.

As Katie was getting ready, on the other side of town, Aaron was getting ready to drive and meet Katie. Aaron heard a knock at his bedroom door.

"Come in," Aaron said.

"So are you ready for your big date?" Sam said. John, upon hearing Sam tease Aaron, came down the hall and into Aaron's room as well.

"Yeah, you going to meet your girlfriend," John said, smiling, walking into Aaron's room.

Aaron laughed. "Ms. Katie and I are just going to get coffee. We are friends."

"Yes, friends from a long, long time ago, I know. You have told us that many times," John said.

"But a friend that you keep a crumpled-up picture of in your sock drawer, along with a picture frame of her as a teenager, which I will say does not look right seeing how you are in your fifties," Sam said, smiling.

Aaron laughed and sat down in a chair, facing Sam and John who were sitting on his bed. "Why are you guys here anyway? Don't you guys have somewhere to be besides hanging out with your dad?"

"Well, John and I decided we were not going to miss this," Sam said, smiling.

"Dad, I don't understand. If you loved Ms. Katie so much, why did you not find her? Why didn't you go after her? I guess I just don't understand," John said.

"It's complicated, and it always was, boys," Aaron said, looking down. "We both had different lives, problems, and issues going on; and when we could, we would spend the little bit of time together that we could."

"You could have had more of those times and lived them for how long now, forty years. What stopped you?" Sam asked.

"I didn't want to go through what I did with your mom again or the few girlfriends I had after. It always seemed to not work out."

"I know I'm still young, but the way you talk about Ms. Katie and you, it seemed like a sure thing to me. Like some kind of telepathic weird love. Or at least that is how you made it sound," John questioned.

"John," Aaron said, laughing, "do you listen to everything I say?"

"Actually, no, I don't," John said, smiling. "But I think Sam and I have this higher-than-normal expectation of love because of you and Ms. Katie. How are we supposed to trust in love if the relationship didn't work out, the one that you said was perfect?"

John did have a point. Aaron knew it, and he knew it was time to tell the boys the truth.

"Katie is special. She always will be to me. I have missed her almost every day since we were teenagers. I will love her until I take my last breath, boys. She has always been the one, even though through the years I tried to replace that love. I just know, and I wish I could tell you better than that. It is just a feel. She does something to my heart each time I hug her or kiss her."

"Gross, Dad," John said, laughing with Sam.

Aaron laughed. "She always has a way of calming me, no matter what part of my life I was at. I was scared too. I did not want to get crushed if Katie walked out of my life again. Not saying they were all her fault. We both just didn't trust in our love, and I think that part is the scariest because each of us at different times walked away."

"What happened the last time you saw her? You said you had a great time seeing each other, but you two stopped talking again. Why?" Sam asked.

Aaron took a deep breath and began to tell Sam and John how Katie and he started communicating again.

Aaron said, "Well, about eight years ago, I was at home with you boys . . ." Aaron had tried to text message Katie two months prior, and Katie did not answer him. Aaron thought that Katie did not want to speak with him anymore. Aaron thought it was finally over, that he had lost Katie forever. But two months later, he received a text message from Katie. When Aaron looked down at his phone, his stomached dropped;

it was Katie. As they began to speak, Aaron's emotions that he had for so long started to surface again. He had been in a dark place for the last three years, and somehow, Katie's few messages had started to pick him up some. Aaron began thinking about Katie daily and would text her often, but he began to worry that Katie was not interested in him as he always had to start conversations with her. It seemed that he was pushing and maybe too hard on Katie. She had just got divorced from a long marriage, and Aaron could tell Katie wasn't herself at times. When Aaron learned that he had to go overseas again, he told Katie he may have to leave but never told Katie goodbye or when he was going. He figured that Katie needed the space and needed the time to be on her own. Aaron hoped that when he got back, Katie and he would remain the way they were for the last two months, but he did not know. He knew Katie was special, and he knew that there would be other men wanting Katie's attention, and he could not give Katie the attention that she deserved. So Aaron left without telling Katie bye, without warning her. Aaron thought it was probably the last time he would talk to Katie, but he hoped it would not be. He hoped when he was in a better space emotionally, it would change. Aaron did not want to keep going overseas, and he knew that he wanted to be with Katie more. Just the timing was off; and instead of explaining it to Katie, because Katie would want to stay with him through it all and it was not fair to her, Aaron left without saying goodbye.

He went overseas for a contract. He didn't know how long, but he knew it was what he needed to do. Aaron thought he could work on himself while overseas and be in a better place once he got home. He had to do it; this was what he wanted. It was what he begged to get back. It was what Aaron asked for many times—a chance to change the outcome of his life with Katie. He just wished with everything in him Katie would somehow know he was doing everything for their future.

Aaron being overseas was nothing new to him. He was realizing as he got older even more, he just couldn't do what he once could. He knew his time was coming to an end, but he did not know how to handle it. Since he was a teenager, Aaron had been either in the military or working on contracts; it was a lifestyle, but now, he had to set it down. He would have to start a new journey soon, like other people he knew. The new life that was so hard for so many guys like him. It scared him because people like him either did well or fell into a dark place, to which he lost some of them to suicide. Aaron believed he would make it though. He had his boys, and as long as he had them, everything would be okay.

Aaron thought about Katie a lot too. His boys were his life, and even Katie would understand that. So many people before her didn't, and Aaron knew he did not want his boys to see him with women coming in and out all the time. He did not want his boys to be meeting several women each month or each year when it didn't work out. Aaron knew Katie was all about Emma and that Katie believed in family, but it still was in his mind. However, if Aaron listened to what his intuition was telling him, he knew that it would be alright with Katie. He just had to stop thinking with his head and start listening to what his body deep down was telling him, but at the time, Aaron couldn't.

A month into it, Aaron logged onto the computer and pulled up his email. While scrolling through them, there was an email from Katie. His heart dropped, and he thought the email was going to go one of two ways: Katie was either going to be pissed or going to be normal Katie. As Aaron opened the email and read the first lines, it was Katie being Katie, the sweet Katie that Aaron knew. It brought back so many emotions, and Aaron could not help but feel loved and missed in Katie's email. Aaron missed Katie too; he always did when they weren't together. The email gave him faith that everything was going to be okay between them, especially with these simple words: "I will be here when you get back. No matter how long it is." He emailed Katie back after reading her email twice, taking in everything she wrote. Aaron knew Katie loved him, but he didn't know if it was enough.

Aaron spent the next week in the field doing stuff that most people would not understand and would never believe if he told anyone. He was tired; he was hurting. Although exhausted, he logged on the computer, hoping to see an email from his Katie. Of course, Katie had emailed him back. Aaron read the email and emailed Katie back. He laid down but could not shut off his mind to thoughts of the boys, to what he just went through, and then of course to thoughts of his Katie. He had to put Katie away—put her away from his mind where it needed to be until he came home to her. It was the only way to ensure his safety and the safety of those with him. It is what he had done ever since he began his military career. It made it a little easier for Aaron to deal with the life he was living.

For the next two months, Aaron did not check his email. He did the job that needed to be done and lived that life free of the boys and Katie. It was what made it a little easier, and it kept him from missing all of them. Until Aaron finally heard he was traveling to go home.

As soon as Aaron flew to his first stop before coming home, he spoke with the boys who were excited Dad was coming home, and he messaged Katie, telling her he was on his way home. Katie messaged him a little and asked when he got settled in if she could see him. Of course, Aaron said yes, although seeing Katie was the last thing on his mind. He was exhausted, trying to process coming back home and switching his mindset from fight to family man. It was hard to transition in the first days and weeks coming home, but somehow, he managed to do it every time.

Aaron made it home early in the morning that next Sunday. After getting up later that morning, Aaron and the boys stayed close by each other. Although worn out, Aaron was in dad mode, playing, laughing, and talking with the boys. In the evening, Aaron messaged Katie, letting her know he made it home. One of the first things Katie asked was about the boys, and she asked if they were excited to see him. Aaron knew Katie got it but still did not know what to do.

He did know that he wanted to see Katie, and he asked if Katie wanted to meet for coffee. Although Katie had a meeting, they were going to make it work. They were going to meet early in the morning at Katie's house after the kids were at school. Aaron drove up to see Katie, and when he pulled up to Katie's house, he was excited and nervous at the same time. He hid his nerves behind his smile and calm demeanor. When Katie opened the door and he stepped in, he was face-to-face with her, the woman he had thought about for ten years. He stood there and just looked at Katie; he could not believe he was in the same room as her. Something he never thought he would do again. He managed to ask for a hug, and Katie willingly hugged him back. Aaron embraced Katie for the first time in ten years. He felt the strong connection they once had, and his heart started beating harder with excitement.

As he listened to Katie talk on her meeting, he stared at her from behind, as she had her back turned to him. Once the meeting was complete, Katie turned and smiled. Aaron had to hug Katie again, to feel her next to him. Somewhere between the hug and the brief time they had seen each other, they kissed. Aaron felt the love with Katie in that moment. He felt every bit of emotion, every bit of love that they had for each other. Nothing had changed between the two, and Aaron knew at that moment it never would. When it was time for him to leave, he did not want to leave but knew he had to. As he was leaving, he turned back toward Katie one more time, taking in the sight of her. He wished this was not the last time he would see her for a while, but deep down, he thought it might be.

"And that was the last time you saw her?" John asked.

"Yeah, it was," Aaron said.

"Why?" Sam asked.

"I don't know. Sometimes you meet people that you love so much that they make you crazy. They make you feel like you are losing control, and you worry about losing that control. Katie is that person for me, and honestly, I know I am that person for Katie. Between the fear of that, taking care of you boys, Katie just getting divorced, and everything else that I needed to fix in my life, I stopped talking to her. Then I went back overseas right before you boys went to see your grandparents for the summer, and I thought that was my fate. I was just happy with the memories of her and the new memory I had to hold on to."

"That makes no sense, Dad," John said finally.

"You both will understand one day, or I hope you do. It is the best feeling yet the scariest feeling," Aaron told the boys.

"What made you decide to text her, what, yesterday? You guys don't waste time, do you?" Sam muttered.

"Just because I walked away didn't mean that I never thought about Katie again. I thought of her a lot and the history between us. I am finally at a good place, a point in my life where I can be who Katie needs and who I want to be with her."

"You wasted like forty years, Dad. You could have done it with her. We could have had a sister," Sam said.

"I could have, but it was my thinking, and we turned out all right, didn't we? Plus, you guys wanted to move to Alaska. Katie was not moving to Alaska, and I knew that. She had to heal from her divorce, and she had so much she wanted to still do. I didn't want to stop her from reaching the goals she had."

"If she is just a friend, why wouldn't she want to see a friend?" John muttered.

Aaron smiled. "You boys know I've always thought of her more than a friend. It was just a title we used, or I used. It made things a little easier, and it didn't confuse you kids. Katie and I both knew we could never just be friends."

Sam smiled. "We were smarter than you think. We knew but really didn't care. You always kept any of your girlfriends away from us."

Aaron looked down at his watch. "I got to go. I don't want to be late."

"You're not going to be late. You are always early for these meetings. I think John and I both have faith that it is going to work out this time."

"It's just coffee, boys."

"We know. Just coffee, just friends, just talking," John mocked.

Aaron stood up, hugging the boys. "I love you, guys."

Aaron grabbed his car keys and walked to the door, turning around right before he left to see the boys. He had raised two strong, good-hearted men; he felt they were his biggest accomplishment.

Sam looked at Aaron. "It's okay to be happy now, Dad."

Aaron turned around and walked outside. He got into his car and drove off, heading to the coffee shop Katie and he agreed to meet at.

⸻

Katie was grabbing her purse and car keys to leave.

Emma smiled. "Are you ready to do this?"

"Yeah, it's just coffee, and it's Aaron."

"I know," Emma said, hugging Katie. "It's going to work this time. You two are soulmates."

Katie only smiled; she didn't fight it with Emma.

Katie walked outside and got into her car, pulling out, heading toward the coffee shop.

As Aaron and Katie drove to the coffee shop, both of their minds were on the last forty years. Forty years of love, forty years of memories. Both were excited to see each other, but both were also nervous. They had no doubt after so long that the chemistry between them would be there, but the question was could they make it work this time? Deep down both knew they wanted to try again; they wanted to make it work, but could they with the history between them? The two had both stayed single since their last meeting, desiring for the other to come back. They knew it was time. They had been in love with each other now way longer than they weren't. It was the only true love either one of them had known.

Katie pulled up to the coffee shop. She guessed Aaron was already inside. She got out of her vehicle and started walking toward the door. Aaron, already sitting inside, looked out of the window just as Katie was walking up to the coffee shop and caught a glimpse of her. His heart started to pound, and a surge of emotions came over him. To him, she looked the same as she did forty years ago.

Katie opened the door to the coffee shop and searched around. She saw Aaron sitting in a booth. She locked eyes with him and smiled as she walked toward him. When she reached the booth, he stood up. They stared at each other.

"Hey, Katie," Aaron said, smiling.

"Hey, you." Katie smiled back at Aaron.

"I think I need a hug."

Katie leaned up to put her arms around Aaron's neck. Aaron picked Katie up, and they embraced. They did not care who was watching. Both needed and deserved the hug after eight years of needing each other. Aaron put Katie back down, and both slid into the booth, sitting across from each other.

CHAPTER 20

Katie and Aaron stared at each other.

Katie smiled. "Hi."

"Hey, you."

"How can you look exactly the same?"

Aaron laughed. "I don't think so, but I'm glad you think so. I'm slower, older, and a lot grayer."

Katie laughed. "Yeah, but the grayer the better."

"If you say so." Aaron grinned. "What have you been up to, Katie?"

"Well, nothing much. Emma is off in college now doing the art thing. I have been writing. I am trying to compose one book a year, so I have been on a tight schedule with that. Hanging out at the house. I did buy a house by the water. I don't know if you knew that."

"I think I read something like that in an article."

"Other than that, I am pretty boring. I am homebody with the dogs. Nothing has changed since the last time. What about you?"

"Sam is in the military. He thinks he has found the one. It's been interesting. John, well, I'm not sure what he wants to do. He's a good kid, just undecided."

"I can relate at that age. You remember I had no clue either."

"Well, you are some big-time author now. The last time I talked to you, you were thinking about writing or wanting to write another book."

"Yeah, I've written six books since then."

"I know," Aaron said.

"You been keeping tabs on me, Aaron?"

"Let's just say I know you made it as an author. By the way, your first fiction book, *Whispered Promises*, seemed familiar to another story I either read or lived."

Katie laughed. "It's a fiction story with the outline of the story being the same as past events in my life."

"The guy in the story, I don't know what he was thinking. I would have scooped that girl up and kept her."

"I think they had to go their separate ways at times in their life to learn a lot of lessons."

"It seems that they did. Seems like the lessons they had to learn were a lot longer than most."

"Well, Aaron, that is what makes the ending so special, because they made it. They both got to experience unconditional love. Their reward from above."

"Yeah, but they missed out on so much love."

"Not really. Maybe being together, but the love was always there."

"I agree there."

"Tell me what the last eight years looked like for you."

"It was just me and the boys. I finished my last contract like I told you I was going to, and me and the boys moved to Alaska for a few years. The boys decided that was not the life they wanted to live, so we moved back to Florida. I taught for a few years, and now, I am just living on my land and living in peace and quiet."

"You moved back to Florida? Where?" Katie said, surprised.

"I live on the outskirts of Jacksonville. I've been there for about six years now."

"Why didn't you tell me? We have been that close for over six years. I can't believe I haven't seen you."

"I am good at keeping to myself and blending in."

"You are over six feet. You don't just blend in, Aaron." Katie and Aaron laughed. "You didn't want to find out what was going on with me?"

"I did, but it had been so long, and I didn't want to interfere in your life. You had just started to get recognized as an author, and you didn't need the confusion. Trust me, I wanted to, Katie. The longer I stayed away, the more I didn't want to walk back into your life and mess up things. I didn't know if you were married again or with someone. It was just better to stay away."

"I would have liked to see you, Aaron. I wish you would have said something. I thought you were still in Alaska. I had no clue you were here."

"I'm sorry, Katie. I curse the decisions I've made at times, but at the time, I thought it was the right thing to do."

Katie sat in silence and then said, "I get it, just a shock."

"Are you married or dating?" Aaron asked suddenly.

Katie rolled her eyes. "No, I have too high standards for anyone."

Aaron laughed. "Why doesn't that surprise me, but high standards, huh?"

Katie smiled. "Yeah."

"Tell me what these high standards are so I can have an idea of what I need to do to get to those standards."

Katie looked Aaron in the eyes. "They weren't you." Aaron looked shocked as Katie continued, "After I saw you the last time, I knew I wanted no one else. I wanted us more than I feared getting hurt. So I waited for you to come back. I knew you would. I just had a feeling, and the next time you did come back, I knew I didn't want to have anything standing in our way. I was done. I just didn't think it would be eight years. I analyzed everything about that day, Aaron, wondering for a long time what I did wrong."

Aaron cut Katie off. "You did nothing wrong, Katie."

Katie continued, "Well, I thought I did for a long time. After a while, I gave up waiting and just decided it wasn't meant to happen in this life. At least I had all the memories, and I've held on to each one of them. I got to know though, Aaron, why did you run the last time?"

Aaron was staring at Katie. Katie had never been so blunt about her feelings and thoughts for Aaron. She had talked about them a little but never so honestly.

"I was scared, Katie. Scared of getting hurt, scared of you settling for me because of the spot you were in. I felt that you needed time and space. Then when I saw you, all the chemistry and the emotions, it was too much for me. I wasn't ready to lose control, and I knew I would with you. I was then and now so in love with you. I just couldn't tell you."

Katie began to tear up. "Aaron, I was scared too. You were never last—you were always first. I told you many times, no one made me feel the way you did. I get it, Aaron, don't get me wrong, but still, we could have made it work. I know everything happens for a reason, but I try and think why, why again. Maybe I wouldn't have become the author I am. Maybe goals would have changed. The sad part is, I didn't contact you again because I thought you had made up your mind and I wasn't for you anymore."

Seeing Katie get upset brought tears to Aaron's eyes. "Katie, it was never you. I had so much going on mentally, with my ex-wife, and I feared losing the boys. I did not want to bring you into my problems, especially when you were starting a writing career. I am so sorry I made you feel that way. Katie, you were and always are special to me." Aaron grabbed Katie's hand, sliding on the other side of the booth next to her. "I love you, Katie. I always have and always will." Aaron hugged Katie. Katie embraced him and laid her head on his shoulder.

"Katie, I have screwed up a lot of things. I think we both have, but one thing I know is I need you in my life and that I love you. I knew it the first day I met you. There was just something about you."

"I wrote you every day you were overseas."

Aaron pulled away from Katie, looking her in the eyes and holding her hands. "I know you did. You will never know how much that meant to me. It gave me something to look forward to. It made me fight harder to get home."

"No, before we met the last time. When I wrote you that first time and you said you were overseas, I didn't have the address, so I bought a journal, and I wrote you every day in it until you came back. I planned to give it to you when I saw you again, but I didn't that day. I thought I would see you again soon, so I continued to write in it. I don't know, maybe to log every time I was thinking of you. I wrote in it until I filled all of the pages." Katie reached in her purse, took out the journal, and handed it to Aaron. Aaron took the journal from her and flipped through the pages that contained Katie's handwriting. He was shocked that Katie had done that for him. Aaron loved Katie even more in that moment as he held the journal, knowing that she continued to write to him long after he had stopped talking to her, knowing with every page she wrote, she had faith that one day she would be able to give it to him.

"I wanted forever, Aaron. The fairy tale I wanted was with you."

"What about now, Katie?"

"I am still missing the last piece of my fairy tale. But right now, I will settle for let's see how it goes. Let's get past this first time seeing each other and make it to a second meeting."

"Katie, I will make it up to you. Just give me that chance. I can be what you need."

"A chance? Aaron, I will always come back to you no matter what happens between us. Aaron, you always were what I needed. You just didn't see it."

Aaron touched Katie's face, pulling her bangs away from her eyes. He slid his hand to her cheek and kissed Katie's lips. "You want to get out of here and go for a drive?" Aaron asked with a smile.

Katie grinned back at Aaron. "Yeah."

Katie and Aaron got into his car and drove off. He parked on the side of the road. The two got out of the vehicle and sat under a large oak tree. Katie laid her head down in Aaron's lap. Aaron began running his fingers through Katie's hair as they sat there and just talked. They would stay there until it was dark, not wanting to leave each other, but having trust in each other that both were done running from their feelings.

In the coming months, both Aaron and Katie kept their word. The first few months had scared them both, but they remained together, not leaving each other's side. They would only look at the past remembering all of the great memories—looking forward to the future they were creating together.

"You two are so cute together." Katie, Aaron, and the kids, now adults, went to a friend of Aaron's retirement party. Katie was curled up in Aaron's lap with her head on his shoulder.

"Thanks," Katie said.

"You two seem so close. How did you meet?"

Katie leaned away from Aaron and looked at him. "You didn't tell them?" Katie said, surprised.

Aaron's friends looked on, confused.

"I figured you could sound like the crazy one," Aaron said, laughing. Katie rolled her eyes, turning back toward the group of Aaron's friends staring at them intently, wanting to know more.

"Well," Katie said, laughing. "I've known Aaron since we were teenagers."

"Really?"

As the friends listened intently, Katie told the story—the story of Aaron and her meeting for the first time, staying in contact through the years, and the love story that unfolded over the past forty years. It was hard to believe that a love story would have so many turns, but Katie and Aaron knew since they were teenagers the love they had for each other. They kept faith in each other and trusted that each would come back to the other.

Life is made up of moments in which we make choices on a direction in our life, hoping the path chosen leads us to our purpose and our soulmate. William Shakespeare once wrote, "The course of true love never did run smooth." Love worth having is messy and teaches us lessons, preparing us for what is waiting on the other side. Trust in the journey with all its bumps and curves. With faith, you will find your fairy tale in the end.

www.ingramcontent.com/pod-product-compliance
Lightning Source LLC
Chambersburg PA
CBHW020610250626
47154CB00004B/1448